ULTIMATE
CHARACTER GUIDE
NEW EDITION

Written by
Melanie Scott

INTRODUCTION

The DC Universe is filled with incredible Super Heroes, dastardly super-villains, and superpowered teams. Get to know more than 200 of these characters and teams in this book. Entries are organized alphabetically according to the first letter of the first word in their name or title. For example, Alfred Pennyworth is under "A," Black Lightning is "B," and Doctor Sivana is "D."

ADAM STRANGE
INTERPLANETARY TRAVELER

Mild-mannered archaeologist Adam Strange is suddenly teleported to the planet Rann by Zeta-Beam technology. Here, he falls in love with Alanna, daughter of top scientist Sardath, and becomes a Super Hero using Rann's amazing technology. The Zeta Beams move Strange between Earth and Rann against his will, meaning that his time with Alanna is always limited.

HUD (Heads-Up Display) in his helmet keeps Strange informed of potential threats and atmospheric conditions

POWERS

Adam Strange has no powers on Earth. When transported to Rann, however, he can use the advanced technology there to perform all kinds of feats. He wears a space suit with a jet pack and life-support systems for moving through space and carries a laser pistol. Adam can also create hard-light shields and weapons with his Holo-Blasters.

Although Strange prefers to solve problems peacefully, he is skilled with various weapons

SMASH

DUEL WITH DESPERO

Adam Strange and his friend Hawkman discover that the super-villain Despero is behind the attacks on the planet Rann. Worse still, Despero is building a Zeta-Beam portal that will allow him to teleport his armies anywhere in the universe. While Hawkman uses every ounce of his strength battling Despero, Strange manages to destroy the portal.

VITAL STATS

REAL NAME Adam Strange

OCCUPATION Super Hero, academic

HEIGHT 6 ft (1.83 m)

WEIGHT 175 lb (79 kg)

BASE Canada; Rann

MAIN ALLIES Alanna Strange, Justice League, Hawkman

MAIN FOES Despero, Byth

ADRIANNA TOMAZ
BLACK ADAM'S QUEEN

Adrianna Tomaz is a refugee brought to Black Adam's court in Kahndaq. She is outspoken about what she considers to be his bad choices. She wants Black Adam to put his people's welfare before his desire for power and his rivalry with foreign Super Heroes. Adam is so impressed with Adrianna that he gives her a magical amulet that bestows superpowers.

Adrianna always wears her magical amulet

POWERS

Adrianna gains superpowers when she holds a mystical amulet. She gains super-strength, speed, and durability. She can fly and heal wounds. Adrianna also has elemental powers and is able to summon wind and storms, among other natural phenomena.

Adrianna is very agile in combat

ROYAL WEDDING

Adrianna Tomaz makes quite an impression on Black Adam. She teaches him to look at life in a different way, and the people of his kingdom of Kahndaq love her for it. After just a few weeks, Adrianna agrees to become Adam's queen. The change in Black Adam himself is clear from his choice of witnesses he wants at the wedding—former foes Shazam and Mary Marvel.

ALFRED PENNYWORTH
LOYAL SERVANT

Alfred Pennyworth is more than just Bruce Wayne's butler. Ever since Bruce was a child, Alfred has been both an advisor and friend (as well as making sure that Bruce eats properly). When Bruce becomes Batman, Alfred is worried for him but helps in any way he can, including cleaning the Batcave!

Suit gives Alfred the appearance of a mild-mannered butler, but villains should not underestimate this former secret agent!

DECOY BATMAN

When the misguided metahuman calling himself Gotham threatens to destroy the city, Batman asks Alfred to do him a very special favor. Alfred will become Batman—just for a short time—to distract Gotham and give the real Dark Knight enough time to save the day. Putting on the Batsuit and driving the Batmobile, Alfred ponders the many challenges he must face in looking after Bruce Wayne.

As a former military man, Alfred is just as comfortable handling a firearm as a tea tray

VITAL STATS

REAL NAME Alfred Pennyworth

OCCUPATION Butler

HEIGHT 6 ft (1.83 m)

WEIGHT 160 lb (73 kg)

BASE Gotham City

MAIN ALLIES Batman, the Bat-Family, Julia Pennyworth

MAIN FOES The Joker, Hush, Court of Owls

POWERS

Alfred's life before he became a butler gave him many useful abilities. His time in the army taught him hand-to-hand combat, marksmanship, and basic medical skills. Later, going into acting, he became an expert in disguise and learned spycraft while working as a British secret agent.

AMANDA WALLER

SUICIDE SQUAD CHIEF

Amanda Waller is a terrifying government agent in charge of the secretive black ops unit named Task Force X, a.k.a. the Suicide Squad. Waller is nicknamed "the Wall," as she is tough and has no compassion for her team. The Suicide Squad members know that she will knock them out if they step out of line or disagree with her.

It is very rare to see a smile on Waller's face

POWERS

Amanda Waller may not have any superpowers, but she is still one of the most feared people in the world. Ruthless, cold, and intimidating, Waller will sacrifice almost anything for the mission. Waller is not well known to the public, but she is powerful and influential behind the scenes.

IRON WILL

When Amanda Waller is questioning evil super-villain Maxwell Lord, he uses his mind control ability on her. Lord forces Waller to reveal classified information, until she manages to shake off his control. Waller attacks him, and Lord remarks that she is the first person who has ever managed to break away from his influence.

Waller always wears a smart suit to work

AMAZO
POWER REPLICATOR

Dr. Armen Ikarus is an expert in diseases at LexCorp. Unfortunately, he becomes the first victim in an outbreak of the Amazo Virus. Lex Luthor modeled this disease on the original Amazo android, hoping to dampen the abilities of metahumans. Ikarus mutates into Amazo, losing his intelligence and becoming a rampaging brute with powerful abilities.

Amazo is much bigger than his original human host

HACKED

The Justice League is in trouble when a bounty is put on the team members' heads. Several super-villains, including Amazo, team up and attack them. In the end, Amazo is defeated by a schoolgirl named Lily and her tablet computer. Lily creates a computer program that can hack into and change Amazo's body and mind. She makes him believe the other super-villains are the Justice League!

POWERS

Amazo can instantly evolve to replicate the metahuman powers of any individual he meets. He can also telepathically communicate with any other carriers of the Amazo virus. In addition to being able to copy powers, he can also give powers to others or weaken powers in metahumans.

VITAL STATS

REAL NAME Armen Ikarus

OCCUPATION Super-villain, former LexCorp employee

HEIGHT 8 ft (2.44 m)

WEIGHT 485 lb (220 kg)

BASE Metropolis

MAIN ALLIES Fearsome Five, Giganta

MAIN FOES Justice League

ANIMAL MAN
AVATAR OF THE RED

As Animal Man, Buddy Baker has to juggle his heroic adventures with his family life as a husband and father. He also discovers that his daughter Maxine has inherited his abilities and may be destined to become even more powerful than him. Until then, Animal Man is the chosen avatar of the Red, the elemental force connecting all animals in the universe.

Animal Man will not wear leather, or any other animal-derived material

Animal Man sometimes struggles to find a place to keep important items, like his house keys

POWERS

Animal Man can use the natural abilities of any animal, accessed through his connection to the Red. This means that he can fly like a bird, swim as easily as a fish, and even possess qualities of extinct animals, like the strength of a Tyrannosaurus Rex.

ALIEN POWER

Animal Man finds himself stranded on a strange planet, surrounded by dangerous-looking aliens, including one that is very large and very powerful. He discovers that his Earth powers are inaccessible but then realizes that he can instead channel the powers of the alien beasts. After taking the power of the big alien, Animal Man is the last being standing.

VITAL STATS

REAL NAME Bernhard "Buddy" Baker

OCCUPATION Super Hero, actor

HEIGHT 5 ft 11 in (1.80 m)

WEIGHT 172 lb (78 kg)

BASE San Diego, California

MAIN ALLIES Justice League, Swamp Thing

MAIN FOES Anton Arcane, Brother Blood

ANTI-MONITOR
THE ULTIMATE DESTROYER

The Anti-Monitor is a being from the Anti-Matter Universe. Formerly known as Mobius, he becomes merged with the destructive force of the Anti-Life Equation. The pain this causes him turns him into a vicious destroyer of entire universes and worlds, including Earth-3, home of the evil Crime Syndicate.

END OF THE ANTI-MONITOR

Darkseid's daughter Grail lures the Anti-Monitor to Earth by telling him that he will be free of the Anti-Life Equation if he kills Darkseid there. In a titanic and destructive battle, Darkseid is killed, and the Anti-Monitor is freed to become Mobius again. But Grail tricks him by transferring the Anti-Life Equation into Steve Trevor and blasting Mobius with Anti-Life Energy, killing him, too.

Anti-matter energy surrounds the Anti-Monitor

The Anti-Monitor's armor stores the energy he absorbs for later use

POWERS

Mobius has superhuman levels of strength, stamina, and durability. But when Mobius becomes the Anti-Monitor, he gains almost unstoppable powers of destruction. He consumes energy from the worlds he destroys. He can also use Anti-Life powers to control any living beings and make them fight for him.

VITAL STATS

REAL NAME Mobius

OCCUPATION Destroyer of Universes

HEIGHT Variable

WEIGHT Variable

BASE Mobile

MAIN ALLIES Grail

MAIN FOES Darkseid, Crime Syndicate, Monitor

AQUALAD
SON OF MANTA

Jackson Hyde grows up unaware of his true origins. His mother is from the undersea kingdom of Xebel, and his absent father is the super-villain Black Manta. What he does know is that he has amazing superpowers that enable him to control water. As he embarks on a new life as the latest Aqualad, Hyde must wrestle with his conflicted identity at the same time as fighting villains.

VITAL STATS

REAL NAME Jackson Hyde
OCCUPATION Super Hero
HEIGHT 6 ft 1 in (1.85 m)
WEIGHT 190 lb (86 kg)
BASE Titans Tower, San Francisco
MAIN ALLIES Teen Titans
MAIN FOES Black Manta

Arm markings glow when Aqualad uses his powers

POWERS

Like all Atlanteans, Aqualad can live underwater and is super-strong, fast, and tough. His hearing and vision are also at superhuman levels. Jackson can generate electricity and shape water with his mind, powers that come from his Xebellian heritage.

Hydrosuit is a hand-me-down from Robin

BOY VS. SHARK

It is Jackson Hyde's dream to join the Teen Titans, but when he arrives at Titans Tower, Robin (Damian Wayne) turns him down. Hyde follows the team when they are called out to battle King Shark. He proves his worth by rescuing Robin from the villain's clutches. Robin admits that Hyde may prove useful and allows him to stay.

Aqualad can use these hilts as bases to create water construct weapons

AQUAMAN
KING OF THE SEAS

Arthur Curry's father is human, but his mother is from the undersea kingdom of Atlantis. As Aquaman, Arthur has a foot in both worlds. He is a Super Hero and member of the Justice League and a sometime ruler of an ancient underwater realm. Aquaman is an extremely powerful being, both on land and in the sea.

VITAL STATS

REAL NAME Arthur Curry

OCCUPATION King of Atlantis, Super Hero

HEIGHT 6 ft 1 in (1.85 m)

WEIGHT 325 lb (147 kg)

BASE Amnesty Bay; Atlantis

MAIN ALLIES Justice League, Mera

MAIN FOES Black Manta, Orm, Dead King

Trident of Neptune is a lethal weapon that is also a symbol of the rulers of Atlantis

Aquaman's armour is in traditional Atlantean colors

Golden belt displays Aquaman's insignia

POWERS

Aquaman has both super-strength and super-speed and is physically capable of living deep underwater with no ill effects. He is an incredibly fast swimmer and can mentally influence the behavior of sea animals. Aquaman can use his trident to channel magical powers.

FAMILY FEUD

Aquaman's half brother Orm, a.k.a. Ocean Master, leads an Atlantean invasion of the surface world, forcing Aquaman to choose between his people and the Justice League. He defeats Orm then asserts his authority over the Atlanteans as their king, ordering them to stop their attack.

ARES
GOD OF WAR

A res is the Olympian God of War. A powerful being that thrives on carnage, he is hated and feared by even the other Gods. One exception is Aphrodite, who loves him and bears his children, including the terrible twins Phobos and Deimos. After Ares disappears from the world, his children search for him in the hope of freeing him or even replacing him as God of War.

Ares's helmet is ancient Greek in style, topped with ram's horns and carved to have the appearance of skull's teeth

Cloak conceals weapons, allowing Ares to strike without warning

POWERS

As God of War, Ares is skilled in both combat and strategy. Violent emotions make him more powerful, and fights tend to break out whenever he is near. Ares is incredibly strong and an unrivaled master with any kind of weapon.

PRISONER OF WAR

Ares has an insatiable hunger for chaos and conflict that eventually drives him insane. The other Olympian Gods hatch a plan to contain him: Hephaestus, God of the Forge, makes chains, and Aphrodite, the Goddess of Love, puts them on Ares. Finally, he finds peace, and he is imprisoned in a place close to Themyscira in the hope that the world will become more peaceful in his absence.

VITAL STATS

REAL NAME Ares

OCCUPATION Olympian God of War

HEIGHT 6 ft 10 in (2.08 m)

WEIGHT 459 lb (208 kg)

BASE Olympus

MAIN ALLIES Deimos and Phobos

MAIN FOES Wonder Woman

ARSENAL
TROUBLED TITAN

Once Green Arrow's sidekick, Roy Harper is now the hero Arsenal and a member of the Titans team. Roy grows up on a Native American reservation, where he learns his amazing archery skills from his adoptive father Big Bow. Roy has suffered in the past but has learned to put himself back together again with the help of his loyal friends.

Arsenal's signature look is the backward-facing baseball cap

VITAL STATS

REAL NAME Roy Harper
OCCUPATION Vigilante
HEIGHT 5 ft 11 in (1.80 m)
WEIGHT 185 lb (84 kg)
BASE New York City, New York
MAIN ALLIES Titans, Team Arrow
MAIN FOES Cheshire

Belt has plenty of places to store gadgets

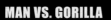

MAN VS. GORILLA

Arsenal has discovered an evil plot by a living, disembodied brain, named Brain, and his talking gorilla associate, Monsieur Mallah. The misguided villains want to take over the world by making Brain the most intelligent being ever. Arsenal is faced with taking them on by himself until the rest of the Titans team arrive and help him save the day.

POWERS

In addition to being one of the world's best archers, Arsenal is skilled in the use of many other weapons. Roy is also an engineering genius. He applies his intellect to inventing a range of trick arrows that can explode, stun, create stasis fields, deploy parachutes, or have a host of other functions.

ARTEMIS
AMAZONIAN OUTLAW

Artemis is one of the Amazons of Bana-Mighdall. She is on a quest to find the fabled Bow of Ra when she runs into Red Hood and Bizarro. Although they make an unlikely team, the three band together in a "Dark Trinity" called the Outlaws. Artemis is a mighty warrior, but even she needs a little help now and again.

VITAL STATS

REAL NAME Artemis
OCCUPATION Vigilante
HEIGHT 6 ft (1.83 m)
WEIGHT 166 lb (75 kg)
BASE Gotham City
MAIN ALLIES The Outlaws
MAIN FOES Black Mask, Circe

POWERS

Like all Amazons, Artemis is exceedingly strong, eternally young, and trained in the use of weapons. She often wields a sword and a magical ax she calls "Mistress," but Artemis's weapon of choice is the Bow of Ra, which is so powerful that a limit to its abilities has not yet been found.

Instead of a heavy helmet, Artemis wears a face guard

Artemis's skill with a bow is symbolized by the arrow symbol on her chest

THE BOW OF RA

The Champion of the Amazons of Bana-Mighdall is the only one worthy enough to wield the Bow of Ra. When Artemis's former friend Akila tries to use the weapon for evil, Artemis takes it from her and fires it. The power of Ra overwhelms Akila, and Artemis becomes the bow's new owner and master of the amazing powers that it brings.

Shin guards provide extra leg protection

THE ATOM
SIZE-CHANGING SUPER HERO

Ryan Choi is a research assistant to Professor Ray Palmer. Choi wants to prove that small things can make a big difference: he gets his opportunity when Palmer lets him in on the secret that he is the Super Hero known as The Atom. Following in his Professor's footsteps, Ryan becomes the latest Atom and is later recruited into the Justice League of America.

The Atom's symbol is a diagram of an atom, with electrons moving in rings around a central nucleus

VITAL STATS

REAL NAME Ryan Choi

OCCUPATION Super Hero, research assistant

HEIGHT 5 ft 8 in (1.73 m)

WEIGHT 160 lb (72 kg)

BASE The Sanctuary, Happy Harbor, Rhode Island

MAIN ALLIES Ray Palmer, Justice League of America

MAIN FOES Chronos

POWERS

Thanks to Professor Ray Palmer's size-changing technology, The Atom can alter his size right down to the subatomic level. He can also change his body mass, increasing it to make himself super-strong, or decreasing it to enable him to fly. Like Palmer, Ryan Choi has a genius-level intellect.

The Bio-Belt changes The Atom's size using the energy of a white dwarf star

CHOSEN HEIR

Ryan Choi dons a size-changing belt and tracks the missing Professor Palmer down in the Microverse. The brave assistant believes that he will have to give up the belt, but Palmer is impressed by Ryan's abilities. He tells Ryan that he has earned the right to wear the suit, giving him his blessing to become The Atom.

ATOM SMASHER
SUPER-STRONG HERO

Albert Rothstein is inspired by his godfather Al Pratt, the original Atom, to become a Super Hero. At first named Nuklon, he later took on the name Atom Smasher! Albert joins the Justice Society of America, but he sometimes struggles to keep to the high standards the team expects. Unfortunately, he inherited some of the super-villain genes of his grandfather, Cyclotron.

VITAL STATS

REAL NAME Albert Rothstein
OCCUPATION Super Hero, scientist
HEIGHT 7 ft 6 in (2.29 m)
WEIGHT 297 lb (135 kg)
BASE New York City, New York
MAIN ALLIES Justice Society of America, Black Adam
MAIN FOES Kobra

Atom Smasher's true identity is concealed beneath a wrestling-style mask

POWERS

Atom Smasher can manipulate the atoms in his body to grow to a great height. He can also increase his mass, making him super-strong and durable. He inherits his metahuman powers from his super-villain grandfather, who gained them by absorbing atomic energy.

THE MEDIATOR

Atom Smasher wants to prove himself to his Justice Society of America teammates. He has his chance when his former friend Black Adam steals the power of Shazam from Billy Batson. Atom Smasher reasons with Adam, telling him that he needs to give up the power before it endangers all his people. His success sees Atom Smasher accepted by the JSA.

ATROCITUS
RED LANTERN LEADER

Atrocitus is the only survivor of the planet Ryut, following an attack by the Manhunters. Driven mad with rage and grief, Atrocitus uses the blood of ancient demons to create a power battery and becomes the first Red Lantern. The Red Lantern Corps are fueled with a desire for vengeance, their blood infused with fury.

POWERS

Atrocitus's red power ring gives him the ability to create red hard-light energy constructs (objects made out of light). It also lets him fly, and he can vomit up toxic burning plasma. Atrocitus's large size, strength, and sharp claws are typical of an individual from Ryut.

Atrocitus's appearance is that of a native of Ryut

VITAL STATS

REAL NAME Atros

OCCUPATION Red Lantern

HEIGHT 7 ft 9 in (2.36 m)

WEIGHT 438 lb (199 kg)

BASE Ysmault

MAIN ALLIES Red Lantern Corps

MAIN FOES Green Lantern Corps

Symbol of the Red Lantern Corps

Red power ring is incredibly difficult to remove

BEST FRIEND

Atrocitus's most loyal lieutenant is the Red Lantern Dex-Starr, a former Earth cat who is mistreated after the death of his owner. His rage at the cruelty is sensed by Atrocitus, who sends a red power ring that Dex-Starr wears on his tail. When Dex-Starr is defeated by Guy Gardner, it is Atrocitus who carries him away to recover and return to fight another day.

AZRAEL
MORAL WARRIOR

Created to be the champion and assassin of the sacred Order of St. Dumas, Azrael finds a new path as part of the Bat-Family. The evil Order forced him to commit terrible deeds in their name, but Azrael manages to break their control over him. A moral and thoughtful man, Azrael now uses his skills in less lethal ways.

Azrael's armor is styled after that of a medieval crusader and is known as the Suit of Sorrows

Azrael's flaming sword is called Murasame

BATMAN A.I.

Ascalon, the A.I. controlling Azrael's suit, decides that Azrael is thinking for himself too much. The A.I. totally takes him over, and Azrael's mind is the setting for an argument between them, while his body fights his friends. Batwing helps Azrael by putting him into a new armored suit, which contains an A.I. based on Batman's personality. The new A.I. breaks into Azrael's mind and gives him the strength to overcome Ascalon.

POWERS

Azrael is a highly trained assassin and an expert with swords, wielding a mystical weapon that bursts into flames. He also wears two wrist gauntlets containing blades. Azrael was made in a laboratory to be a living weapon, so his strength and stamina are heightened above normal human levels.

Bane is one of Batman's most formidable enemies. He is big and super-strong, but Bane is not just a hulking brute. The villain possesses an intellect on par with the Dark Knight himself. Bane grows up alone in a prison cell, serving time for his father's crimes, and resolves that he will conquer all criminals. Over time, he grows in strength until he breaks out of his cell and heads for Gotham City.

Wrestler mask hides Bane's identity

VITAL STATS

REAL NAME Unknown

OCCUPATION Super-villain

HEIGHT 6 ft 8 in (2.03 m)

WEIGHT 350 lb (159 kg)

BASE Peña Duro, Santa Prisca

MAIN ALLIES Rā's Al Ghūl

MAIN FOES Batman, Catwoman, Kobra Cult

ASSAULT ON SANTA PRISCA

Bane returns to his childhood prison, Santa Prisca, but now he lives there as a king. Batman needs help from Psycho-Pirate—Bane's ally who lives on the island—so he leads a raid on Santa Prisca. The Dark Knight takes Psycho-Pirate and leaves Bane furious. The villain swears to come to Gotham City and take his revenge on Batman.

POWERS

Bane spends many years inside a prison cell, all the while honing his body and mind to their peak level. His use of the dangerous chemical Venom gives Bane additional strength, durability, and speed. He can also use Venom to heal wounds. However, if Bane uses too much Venom, he can become mentally unstable.

BATGIRL
BORN TO FIGHT CRIME

Barbara Gordon's father, Commissioner Gordon, believes a career in the Gotham City Police Department is too dangerous for her. Determined to find her own way to fight crime, Barbara becomes a masked vigilante. She wears a costume inspired by Batman and hits Gotham City's streets, armed not with superpowers but with incredible intelligence and tremendous courage.

POWERS

Barbara Gordon has no superpowers, but she possesses a genius-level intellect and a photographic memory. In addition to having expert detective skills, she is an accomplished martial artist and gymnast. Barbara is also a hacker but uses her advanced computer skills for good causes.

ORACLE

Barbara is left wheelchair-bound after being attacked by The Joker, so she uses her computer-hacking talents to fight crime. Now known as Oracle, she searches computer networks and the web for information to help other heroes. A few years later, Barbara is cured of her paralysis, enabling her to resume her career as Batgirl.

Half-cowl masks Batgirl's face but allows her hair to come out at the back

Batgirl's version of iconic bat-symbol is yellow

Loaded with cool gadgets

BATMAN
THE DARK KNIGHT

Batman is the protector of Gotham City and one of the senior members of the Justice League. After his life is scarred by crime, Bruce Wayne adopts the Batman identity to strike fear into the hearts of criminals. He is a master detective and highly skilled in hand-to-hand combat. Batman also uses an incredible range of high-tech crime-fighting equipment.

Cowl gives enhanced vision and hearing and deploys gas if someone tries to remove it

Cape can be used for gliding

VITAL STATS

REAL NAME Bruce Wayne

OCCUPATION Businessman, crime fighter

HEIGHT 6 ft 2 in (1.88 m)

WEIGHT 210 lb (95 kg)

BASE Gotham City

MAIN ALLIES Justice League, the Bat-Family

MAIN FOES The Joker, Rā's al Ghūl, Bane

DARK KNIGHTS

Batman faces a threat worse than any he has faced before when he encounters evil versions of himself from the Dark Multiverse. Known as the Dark Knights, these villains try to invade Earth. Their leader is a Joker-ized Batman, named The Batman Who Laughs. Batman has to team up with The Joker to defeat him.

POWERS

Batman has no superpowers but is able to track down and defeat villains with a dizzying array of gadgets and nonlethal weapons. Access to the vast wealth of Wayne Enterprises ensures that all of his equipment is always at the cutting edge of available technology.

BATWING
ALL IN THE FAMILY

Luke Fox is the son of Wayne Industries CEO Lucius Fox. He has inherited his father's technological genius and his head for business. However, Luke also wants to go into the secret side of the family's line of work—crime fighting. When the first Batwing resigns, Batman gives Luke the role. Batwing's talent for engineering is a great asset to the Bat-Family.

LEAP OF FAITH

Luke proves his worth when the police gala that he is attending with Batman and Batwoman is attacked by a group of villains. The young hero heads to the roof of the building and summons his Batwing suit remotely. As he jumps to the ground, the suit assembles around him, and he is ready for action.

Batwing's suit has a wide range of high-tech features, including invisibility, hologram projection, and medical equipment

POWERS

Batwing is a highly skilled mixed martial artist and an elite-level boxer. His genius for invention and engineering is a perfect fit for the Bat-Family, as gadgets and technology are a big part of its crime-fighting arsenal. One of these gadgets, the Batwing suit, gives Batwing an array of offensive and defensive capabilities.

BATWOMAN
SERVING GOTHAM CITY

Inspired by her cousin Bruce Wayne, socialite and former military academy student Katerine "Kate" Kane is keen to serve the citizens of Gotham City in any way she can. She undergoes a rigorous training process devised by her soldier father, becoming a living weapon named Batwoman.

POWERS

Batwoman does not possess superpowers but has extensive military training and is skilled in several martial arts. Although she is a firearms expert, she prefers to use hand-to-hand fighting, Batarangs, or even a version of the Scarecrow's fear toxin in battle.

Mask contains anti-hypnotism lenses

Trademark red hair is a wig and conceals Kane's identity

THE GOTHAM KNIGHTS

Batman trusts Batwoman so much that he reveals to her that he is really Bruce Wayne, but Kate already knows. He then asks her to use her experience of military boot camp to begin training the next generation of Gotham's heroes—Red Robin, Spoiler, Orphan, and Clayface—named The Gotham Knights.

VITAL STATS

REAL NAME Katherine "Kate" Rebecca Kane

OCCUPATION Crime fighter

HEIGHT 5 ft 11 in (1.80 m)

WEIGHT 141 lb (64 kg)

BASE Gotham City

MAIN ALLIES Batman, Hawkfire, Alice, The Gotham Knights

MAIN FOES Nocturna, Scarecrow, Knife

BEAST BOY
ANIMAL SHAPE-SHIFTER

Beast Boy has the ability to transform into the shape of any living creature and take on its powers. Having lost his parents at a young age, Beast Boy is glad to find a new kind of family with the Teen Titans. He brings an amazing array of animal powers to the roster, as well as some truly terrible jokes.

Beast Boy cannot change his skin color, so his animal forms are always green

VITAL STATS

REAL NAME Garfield "Gar" Logan

OCCUPATION Super Hero

HEIGHT 5 ft 8 in (1.73 m)

WEIGHT 150 lb (68 kg)

BASE Hall of Justice, Washington, D.C.

MAIN ALLIES Titans, Teen Titans

MAIN FOES Deathstroke, Trigon, N.O.W.H.E.R.E.

BIO-HACKED

Beast Boy gets involved with Nevrland, a virtual reality startup offering to show people what they've always dreamed of. For Gar, it is having his parents around ... plus pranking Superman and winning an Oscar. But Nevrland is actually a back door to mind-control, and its creator commands Beast Boy to attack his Teen Titans teammates! Gar eventually overcomes the mind control and returns to his senses.

POWERS

Beast Boy can change his shape to look like any animal that he has seen, even if just in a picture. While in the form of a particular animal, Gar has all its abilities. He is connected to the Red, the elemental force that connects all animal life.

Beast Boy does not tend to wear shoes, as they don't ever fit him

Big Barda is trained from birth by Granny Goodness to become a fearsome soldier. She leads Darkseid's elite warriors, the Female Furies. However, when she falls in love with Scott Free, a.k.a. Mister Miracle, she deserts the Furies. Barda travels to Earth and starts a new life as a hero.

POWERS

As a New God of Apokolips, Big Barda has superhuman strength and durability. Her skills as a warrior are exceptional even for an Apokoliptian. In addition, she also wields one of the most powerful objects in the universe—the Mega-Rod. This mighty weapon gives Barda the ability to teleport.

The indestructible Mega-Rod helps Barda fight even the strongest foes

Apokoliptian armor increases Barda's already awesome durability

STAR-CROSSED LOVERS

Big Barda and Mister Miracle are supposed to be on their honeymoon when the Darkseid War breaks out. When her husband is attacked by the powerful Kanto, Barda easily dispatches the opponent. But later she has to agree to return to the Furies in exchange for the team's help defeating Darkseid's daughter, Grail. Barda leaves a heartbroken Mister Miracle behind.

REAL NAME Big Barda

OCCUPATION Soldier, Super Hero

HEIGHT 7 ft (2.13 m)

WEIGHT 197 lb (89 kg)

BASE Los Angeles, California

MAIN ALLIES Mister Miracle

MAIN FOES Darkseid

BIZARRO
THE CLONE OF STEEL

Bizarro is an imperfect clone of Superman, created by Lex Luthor. He is stolen by Black Mask to be used as a weapon but is rescued by Red Hood and Artemis. He joins them as the third member of the Outlaws team. Bizarro's powers are similar to Superman's, but there are a few striking (and bizarre) differences between them!

POWERS

Like Superman, Bizarro has super-strength and speed and is invulnerable. Unlike the Man of Steel, he has freeze vision and flame breath. Bizarro is also vulnerable to blue Kryptonite, not green—green Kryptonite is actually used by Lex Luthor to bring him back to life.

VITAL STATS

REAL NAME Bizarro

OCCUPATION Vigilante

HEIGHT 6 ft 3 in (1.91 m)

WEIGHT 345 lb (156 kg)

BASE Gotham City

MAIN ALLIES
The Outlaws

MAIN FOES
Black Mask,
Solomon Grundy

Bizarro's gray skin marks him out as an imperfect clone

Bizarro wears a reversed version of Superman's S-shield

BRAINZARRO

After Bizarro apparently sacrifices himself to save his Outlaws teammates, Lex Luthor is able to revive him. However, whereas the old Bizarro was not smart, the revitalized version is dubbed "Brainzarro" by Red Hood. Bizarro quickly devises a range of high-tech new equipment for the Outlaws, including jet packs.

BLACK ADAM
ANCIENT MENACE

Black Adam is an immensely powerful being originally from ancient Egypt. His nephew used to have the magic of the wizard Shazam until Black Adam stole it from him. As Kahndaq's monarch, Black Adam tolerates no challenge to his authority. However, he has been known to fight on the side of good if the Earth itself is threatened.

Costume is a dark version of his nemesis Shazam's costume

POWERS

After switching from his human form to his magically enhanced state, Black Adam is very powerful. His strength, speed, and stamina are at demigod levels. He can also fly, including in space, and fire lightning blasts. In his Black Adam form, he is virtually immortal.

MOVING THE MOON

After the Crime Syndicate's Ultraman pushes the moon to block the sun and make himself more powerful, Black Adam and Sinestro save the day for Earth. The two fly to the moon and use their immense combined strength to push it away. They bring sunlight back to Earth, weakening Ultraman and allowing the captured Justice League to escape.

Insignia shows the lightning bolt of Shazam

VITAL STATS

REAL NAME Teth-Adam

OCCUPATION Ruler of Kahndaq

HEIGHT 6 ft 3 in (1.91 m)

WEIGHT 250 lb (113 kg)

BASE Kahndaq

MAIN ALLIES Council of the Immortals

MAIN FOES Shazam, Council of Eternity, Crime Syndicate

BLACK CANARY
THE POWER OF THE VOICE

Black Canary is a hero with a big voice: her shattering scream is a mighty weapon against anyone foolish enough to fight against her. She is a good strategic thinker and leader, as she has shown as part of several super-teams. She is also a talented musician and vocalist.

VITAL STATS

REAL NAME Dinah Drake-Lance

OCCUPATION Vigilante, former singer

HEIGHT 5 ft 7 in (1.70 m)

WEIGHT 130 lb (59 kg)

BASE Mobile

MAIN ALLIES Justice League of America, Birds of Prey, Team Arrow

MAIN FOES Basilisk, Calculator, Zodiac Master

NEW RECRUIT

When Batman decides to assemble a new Justice League of America to give the public a more mortal, relatable team of heroes, Black Canary is one of the first names on his list. Batman believes that Dinah's honesty, hard work, and willingness to speak out and not care if others disagree are all valuable assets.

Black Canary's leather jacket is the perfect complement to her motorcycle

Steel-toe-capped boots give Black Canary's kicks added impact

POWERS

Black Canary's only metahuman power is her Canary Cry, a scream so loud that its vibrations can destroy any objects they hit. Due to the sheer power of her cry and her concern about hurting innocents, Black Canary tries to win her battles with her impressive martial arts skills first.

BLACK HAND
AVATAR OF THE BLACK

William Hand is a madman. He is chosen by a corrupt Guardian of the Universe to be the living embodiment of a life-destroying force known as the Black. Wearing a black power ring, he is the first Black Lantern, tasked with recruiting many more to the evil Corps. Their mission: to bring Nekron, Lord of the Unliving, to Earth.

POWERS

Black Hand can use his ring to drain the emotional energy from power rings of other colors. As the herald of Nekron, he has the ability to create an army of zombies. He can also absorb the life force of others to heal his own injuries.

Black Hand's symbol was originally the logo for the funeral home his family owns

THE SOURCE WALL RISES

With the New Gods engaged in a war with the Lantern Corps, Green Lantern Hal Jordan recruits Black Hand to help them defeat their mutual immortal enemies. At the edge of the known universe, Black Hand touches the mysterious Source Wall, causing the beings who have been trapped in it to spring to life and attack the New Gods. Black Hand himself eventually becomes a part of the Source Wall.

Black Hand wears a black power ring (though he can access his powers without it)

VITAL STATS

REAL NAME William Hand

OCCUPATION Super-villain

HEIGHT 5 ft 7 in (1.70 m)

WEIGHT 165 lb (75 kg)

BASE Coast City

MAIN ALLIES Black Lantern Corps

MAIN FOES Green Lantern

BLACK LIGHTNING
BRIGHT SPARK

Jefferson Pierce is a very busy man. A dedicated high-school teacher by day, he is Cleveland's own hero Black Lightning by night. Black Lightning may have a strained relationship with local law enforcement, but he has a loyal team that helps him train, and even backs him up on missions. His incredible electrical powers can take down even the toughest gangsters.

Black Lightning's goggles make his face blurry and unrecognizable, both in person and on screens

VITAL STATS

REAL NAME Jefferson Pierce

OCCUPATION Super Hero, teacher

HEIGHT 6 ft 1 in (1.85 m)

WEIGHT 182 lb (83 kg)

BASE Cleveland, Ohio

MAIN ALLIES Ernie and Tommi Colavito, Amberjack, Usagi

MAIN FOES Weathermen, Tobias Whale

Black Lightning's suit shields him from impacts, and can also change to a stealth mode

POWERS

Black Lightning's body can generate and harness electricity, allowing him to create force fields and fire powerful blasts at his opponents. He can also fly using electromagnetism, a technique taught to him by Cyborg. Black Lightning's tech maintains his secret identity and keeps him one step ahead of the criminals.

PROTECTING THE INNOCENT

Tensions are running high after the devious Tobias Whale stirs up trouble between the police and citizens of Cleveland. When two young boys who have an alien-tech gun are cornered by the cops, Black Lightning rushes to the scene. He arrives just in time to use his force field as a shield, preventing the jittery police officers from shooting the frightened kids.

BLACK MANTA
MARINE MENACE

Black Manta is one of Aquaman's deadliest foes. His only desire is to destroy Aquaman, no matter who else gets hurt in the process. Black Manta's battle-suit makes him far more dangerous than a normal human, and his strange, ray-shaped helmet makes him look menacing.

VITAL STATS

REAL NAME David Hyde

OCCUPATION Treasure hunter, criminal

HEIGHT 6 ft 2 in (1.88 m)

WEIGHT 205 lb (93 kg)

BASE Mobile

MAIN ALLIES The Secret Society, Legion of Doom, N.E.M.O.

MAIN FOES Aquaman, Aqualad

Eyes of helmet fire optic lasers and enable Black Manta to see in infrared

Equipment allows Black Manta to breathe underwater indefinitely and protects against pressure changes

POWERS

Though he lacks superpowers, Black Manta is a formidable opponent. He is incredibly intelligent and skilled at fighting with weapons or hand to hand. He is an excellent swimmer, and his physical abilities are raised to superhuman levels by his suit, whether underwater or on land.

FEUDING FAMILY

When Black Manta seeks out his long-lost son Jackson Hyde, a.k.a. Aqualad, he is not looking to be a good father. He just wants to use the boy's necklace to find an artifact called the Black Pearl, which will give Manta total control over the oceans. However, even with the Pearl, Black Manta's power is no match for his son's, and he is defeated.

Armor colored black for camouflage at depth; gives superhuman strength and durability, plus insulation

BLACKHAWK
BLACK OPS COMMANDER

Blackhawk is the code name of Colonel Andrew Lincoln, commander of the Blackhawk Program. His team is set up by the United Nations to respond covertly to threats from new types of technology. Blackhawk is a skilled leader and tactician, although he leaves the tech side to other teammates.

Like all of his team, Blackhawk wears the symbol of the Blackhawk Squadron on his uniform

VITAL STATS

REAL NAME Andrew Lincoln

OCCUPATION Pilot, covert ops commander

HEIGHT 6 ft 1 in (1.85 m)

WEIGHT 95 lb (88 kg)

BASE Blackhawk Island

MAIN ALLIES Blackhawk Program

MAIN FOES Mother Machine, Steig Hammer

REVENGE MISSION

After lives are lost in an attack on the Blackhawks' base, Blackhawk personally leads a mission to take revenge on the perpetrator. Blackhawk orders all staff except his Alpha Team to stand down and takes responsibility for the off-the-books action. If that means being fired at the end of it, so be it. Under his orders, his team successfully capture the mastermind of the attack.

Blackhawk is always well armed and ready for battle

POWERS

Blackhawk lacks superpowers, but he has a huge amount of military experience, including secret black ops. He is an excellent pilot and is skilled in combat and with weaponry. He is made commander of the Blackhawks due to his leadership qualities and tactical knowledge.

BLUE BEETLE
HIGH-TECH BUG

Jaime Reyes has a mystical scarab beetle embedded in his spine that gives him incredible powers. As he is still in high school, he has to try to keep up with his homework while battling villains as the Super Hero Blue Beetle. He is mentored in this by the previous Blue Beetle, Ted Kord.

Blue Beetle has long, angled blades protruding from his back that can strike like insect stings

POWERS

At Jaime's mental command, the scarab inside him produces an armor covering his whole body. The scarab is sentient and communicates with Jaime telepathically, helping him in his fights and missions. The armor can produce a range of weapons and shields, and also deploys wings for flight.

With the scarab armor on, Jaime's identity is completely concealed

MIND LINK

Jamie is at first relieved when the scarab is removed and he can go back to a normal life. But a demon named Arion gains control of the scarab and its powers, intending to use it to end creation itself. Jaime realizes that he still has the power to stop Arion if he summons the scarab telepathically.

VITAL STATS

REAL NAME Jaime Reyes

OCCUPATION Super Hero, high-school student

HEIGHT 5 ft 8 in (1.73 m)

WEIGHT 145 lb (66 kg)

BASE El Paso, Texas

MAIN ALLIES Ted Kord, OMAC, Batman

MAIN FOES Blot, Mordecai Cull

BOOSTER GOLD
HERO FROM THE FUTURE

Born in the 25th century, Michael Jon Carter decides to make a name for himself in the past. He steals technology from his own time and uses it to become a 21st-century Super Hero named Booster Gold. Carter becomes the leader of Justice League International, although the self-obsessed time traveler sometimes struggles to gain respect from his teammates.

Visor allows Booster to see through walls

Wristbands fire energy blasts

SKEETS

Booster Gold is often aided by his robotic sidekick Skeets. A former security robot from the 25th century, Skeets provides Booster with a vast knowledge of 21st-century events to give him an advantage. The robot is also useful in a fight and has a variety of built-in weapons.

VITAL STATS

REAL NAME Michael Jon Carter

OCCUPATION Time traveler, Super Hero

HEIGHT 6 ft 2 in (1.88 m)

WEIGHT 215 lb (98 kg)

BASE Mobile

MAIN ALLIES Justice League International, Batman

MAIN FOES Peraxxus, Deimos

POWERS

Booster Gold's superpowers all come from the futuristic tech he stole from the 25th-century museum where he used to work as a security guard. His power suit gives him superhuman strength and durability, as well as creating a protective force field. He can also travel through time using the Time Sphere.

BRAINIAC
THE COLLECTOR

Brainiac is one of Superman's most formidable foes. He is super-intelligent and dedicated to the pursuit of even greater knowledge. This leads Brainiac to start shrinking entire cities and keeping them in bottles for him to study. However, at times when the entire Multiverse seems to be threatened, Brainiac has been known to help Super Heroes.

Brainiac's head has glowing nerve-ending terminals that harness mental abilities

VITAL STATS

REAL NAME Vril Dox

OCCUPATION Collector, scientist

HEIGHT 6 ft 6 in (1.98 m)

WEIGHT 300 lb (136 kg)

BASE Mobile

MAIN ALLIES Telos

MAIN FOES Superman

Like all Coluans, Brainiac has green skin

CONVERGENCE

Brainiac's curiosity about the Multiverse leads him to visit various crisis points throughout the history of multiple universes. Unfortunately, his journey turns him into a vast, mutated creature. In an attempt to return to normal and prevent the collapse of the Multiverse, he helps the displaced heroes of various realities reset the timeline.

POWERS

Brainiac is a Coluan of 12th-level intelligence, making him one of the most powerful intellects who has ever existed. He is a scientist and inventor, and one of his most famous creations is the technology that enables him to shrink cities and collect them.

BRAINIAC 5
ALIEN GENIUS

Although his ancestors may not have been very heroic, Brainiac 5 is different. He wants to use his amazing super-intelligence to protect those who cannot protect themselves. Brainiac 5 is sometimes arrogant, but he is a valued member of the Legion of Super-Heroes.

Legion Flight Ring enables Brainiac 5 to fly and travel through space

POWERS

Brainiac 5 has what is known as 12th-level intelligence, which marks him out as exceptional even for a Coluan. He has encyclopedic knowledge and is a master of scientific invention. It is Brainiac 5 who comes up with the Time Bubble tech that enables the Legion of Super-Heroes to travel through time.

As a native of the planet Colu, Brainiac 5 has green skin

BEATING A BLACK HOLE

When Brainiac 5 accidentally creates a black hole that threatens to suck in the planet Thanagar, he is determined to use his intelligence to put right his mistake. He comes up with the audacious plan of using Zeta Beams to move Thanagar into the orbit of its neighbor, Rann, and out of range of the black hole.

Brainiac 5's Force Field Belt is his own invention and works only when he is the one wearing it

VITAL STATS

REAL NAME Querl Dox
OCCUPATION Legionnaire
HEIGHT 5 ft 10 in (1.78 m)
WEIGHT 160 lb (73 kg)
BASE Legion Headquarters
MAIN ALLIES Legion of Super-Heroes
MAIN FOES Emerald Empress, Legion of Super-Villains

BRIMSTONE
DEAL WITH THE DEVIL

A sinister character named the Salesman arrives in the rundown town of York Hills. He offers young Joe Chamberlain a deal—become one of his "Agents" and make his home somewhere people want to visit. Joe makes the deal, but it isn't what he expects. He is turned into a fiery demon, named Brimstone. His transformation also destroys York Hills, ensuring people will come to visit the devastation.

Brimstone appears to have fire inside his body, flaming out through cracks in his skin

Brimstone can unleash raging demonic fire on his enemies

ON THE ROAD

After York Hills' destruction, Brimstone and his sister Annie use the Salesman's ledger to track down other towns that the villain plans to annihilate. They come across a monstrous creature named Detritus, another of the Salesman's Agents. Brimstone is still learning to control his new powers but manages to defeat Detritus.

POWERS

Brimstone has an advanced healing factor and is super-strong and durable. At first, Joe finds his new powers are overwhelming and struggles to control them, but over time he learns to master them. Joe can change back into his human form, yet he is warned that his human side may be permanently replaced one day in the future.

BRONZE TIGER
MASTER OF MARTIAL ARTS

Bronze Tiger is a vigilante and former assassin with a shadowy past. What is known for sure is that he is one of the best martial-arts fighters in the world, on par with the deadly Lady Shiva. He is even capable of defeating Batman in hand-to-hand combat. Although his allegiances have been uncertain, it seems he is ready to lend his talents to fighting for good.

Bronze Tiger has tattoos resembling tiger stripes on his head

POWERS

Bronze Tiger is one of the world's foremost martial artists. He has mastered a variety of styles, including aikido, karate, and kung fu. He has also been known to increase his strength to superhuman levels by using the substance Venom.

Necklace of tiger teeth adorns Bronze Tiger's neck

EARNING HIS FREEDOM

Bronze Tiger is part of a team of Arkham Asylum inmates handpicked by Batman for a raid on Bane's island stronghold of Santa Prisca. He is let out and has a brief sparring match with Batman, before agreeing to the mission. After the success of the raid on Santa Prisca, Batman rewards Bronze Tiger with his freedom.

VITAL STATS

REAL NAME Benjamin "Ben" Turner

OCCUPATION Vigilante, former assassin

HEIGHT 5 ft 11 in (1.80 m)

WEIGHT 196 lb (89 kg)

BASE Gotham City

MAIN ALLIES Batman

MAIN FOES Bane

BUMBLEBEE
SIZE-CHANGING SUPER HERO

Bumblebee is a brave Super Hero—even when she's the size of an insect. She is the newest member of the Titans but has already proven herself in battle. Married to the hero Herald, Karen first reveals her powers when nine months pregnant with their child. Bumblebee's first mission with the Titans, to stop Mister Twister, causes her to go into labor!

VITAL STATS

REAL NAME Karen Beecher-Duncan

OCCUPATION Air accident investigator

HEIGHT 5 ft 7 in (1.70 m)

WEIGHT 130 lb (59 kg)

BASE Titans Tower, New York City

MAIN ALLIES Titans

MAIN FOES Mister Twister, Fearsome Five

POWERS

Bumblebee wears an armored exo-suit that gives her protection and the power of flight. She has superhuman speed and can fire energy "stings" with her hands. Bumblebee can also shrink down to the size of an insect.

Quartz eyepieces augment vision

DRAMATIC DEBUT

As the Titans battle the Fearsome Five, they seem to be losing until Bumblebee enters the fight. She shows the villains all the devastating effects of her superpowers. Bumblebee stings, swoops, and shrinks her way to victory.

Biometric exo-suit lets Bumblebee fly and channel her sting powers

CAPTAIN ATOM
NUCLEAR DYNAMO

When a quantum-field experiment goes wrong, it turns Nathaniel Adam into Captain Atom, a being of pure energy. His powers makes him capable of great feats of heroism, but they are very unstable, until a journey into the past gives him greater control.

As Captain Atom, Adam is made of pure energy, though he can now switch to his old human form as well

Captain Atom displays the atom symbol on his chest

BACK TO THE FUTURE

A catastrophic overload of Captain Atom's powers sends him back in time. After five years in the past living a normal life, his powers return, and he is sent back to the present. However, Atom's powers are now more stable, and his appearance has changed. Adam returns to being a Super Hero so that public trust in Captain Atom can be restored.

VITAL STATS

REAL NAME Nathaniel Adam

OCCUPATION Super Hero, government agent

HEIGHT 6 ft 4 in (1.93 m)

WEIGHT 200 lb (91 kg)

BASE The Mesaplex

MAIN ALLIES Doctor Megala

MAIN FOES Ultramax

POWERS

Captain Atom has incredible levels of quantum-powered strength, maintained by constantly drawing on the energy of the quantum field. He can fire energy bolts with pinpoint accuracy at multiple targets. He can also enter the quantum field, where he can become intangible.

CAPTAIN BOOMERANG
BEANIE-WEARING BAD GUY

George "Digger" Harkness, a.k.a. Captain Boomerang, can expertly throw boomerangs with pinpoint accuracy. His customized weapons hit their targets and return to him. He tries to use his talents to become a super-rich criminal but is stopped by The Flash (Barry Allen). Digger ends up in prison and is forcibly recruited into Amanda Waller's Suicide Squad.

Boomerang has sharpened edge

Beanie hat has a boomerang symbol

BACK AGAIN

When General Zod attacks the Suicide Squad, he appears to vaporize Captain Boomerang. However, Boomerang has actually been digitized and is trapped in Belle Reve's computer systems. Harley Quinn electrocutes the rampaging Zod and inadvertently "downloads" and resurrects Digger. Declaring himself General Boomerang, he fires a weapon at Zod, but his boast is squashed when the electrocuted Kryptonian falls on him.

POWERS

Captain Boomerang can do far more than throw boomerangs with unbelievable accuracy. He is an expert at making the weapons and often adds extra features. Some of his trick boomerangs pack electric shocks, hidden lasers, explosives, or even the ability to travel through time!

VITAL STATS

REAL NAME George "Digger" Harkness

OCCUPATION Government black ops agent

HEIGHT 5 ft 9 in (1.75 m)

WEIGHT 167 lb (76 kg)

BASE Belle Reve Penitentiary

MAIN ALLIES Suicide Squad

MAIN FOES The Flash (Barry Allen)

CAPTAIN COLD
ROGUE LEADER

Leonard Snart is Captain Cold and uses an ingenious cold gun. Captain Cold leads his Rogues gang in heists to try to get rich. They are based in Central City and often face The Flash (Barry Allen). After still managing to commit crimes while imprisoned in Iron Heights Penitentiary, Captain Cold is moved to the ultra-secure Belle Reve prison. Then, he is forcibly recruited into the Suicide Squad.

Visor protects Captain Cold's eyes from the flashes discharged by his gun

Cold gun built by Captain Cold himself

PROTECTING EARTH

Earth-3's evil Crime Syndicate travel to Prime Earth and recruit most of its super-villains. Captain Cold and the Rogues reject them, wanting to protect their home Central City. Snart faces Johnny Quick, the Crime Syndicate's evil equivalent of The Flash, and defeats him with his cold gun.

POWERS

Captain Cold's power comes from his cold gun, a weapon he constructed that paralyzes his opponents using an extremely cold beam. For a time, Cold's powers were fused into his DNA, but the villain Deathstorm took this ability away. Cold has now returned to using his cold gun once more.

VITAL STATS

REAL NAME Leonard Snart

OCCUPATION Criminal

HEIGHT 6 ft 2 in (1.88 m)

WEIGHT 196 lb (89 kg)

BASE Central City

MAIN ALLIES The Rogues, Suicide Squad

MAIN FOES The Flash (Barry Allen)

CATWOMAN
PRINCESS OF PLUNDER

Selina Kyle, a.k.a. Catwoman, is the best thief in Gotham City. She is also a self-appointed protector of those living in the city's worst districts. Selina has crossed paths with Batman many times. Even though he disapproves of her crimes, the Dark Knight is drawn to her.

Signature night-vision goggles also enable Catwoman to see security lasers

Gloves have retractable, razor-sharp claws

POWERS

While Catwoman has no superpowers, she is an expert thief and martial artist. She also wields a whip and wears clawed gloves to give her an extra edge. Used to life in Gotham City's roughest streets, Selina Kyle is above all a survivor.

VITAL STATS

REAL NAME Selina Kyle

OCCUPATION Thief, vigilante

HEIGHT 5 ft 7 in (1.70 m)

WEIGHT 138 lb (63 kg)

BASE Gotham City

MAIN ALLIES Batman, Holly Robinson, Rex Calabrese

MAIN FOES Black Mask, Hush, the Penguin

LOVE CAT

In Batman's first encounter with Catwoman, he stops her from stealing a diamond. He then buys the gem, unknown to her, because he felt that he might need it. After years of not-quite romance, Batman decides to ask Catwoman to marry him. He proposes with a ring that has the diamond mounted on it.

THE CHEETAH
FELINE FOE

The Cheetah is one of Wonder Woman's worst enemies, although the two were once good friends. Barbara Minerva taught Wonder Woman the ways of the world when she first arrived from Themyscira. But after her transformation into The Cheetah, Barbara's animal side takes over, and she becomes a danger to Wonder Woman—and many others.

Feline appearance, with yellow eyes, sharp teeth, and pointed ears

POWERS

Since changing into The Cheetah, Barbara resembles a humanoid version of a big cat, and her powers reflect this. She uses her razor-sharp claws to attack with superhuman speed, and she also has superhuman strength. The Cheetah's bite can also turn her victims into cheetahlike beings like herself.

The Cheetah's main weapons are her deadly sharp claws

Skin is completely cheetahlike, with tan-colored fur and black spots

VITAL STATS

REAL NAME
Barbara Ann Minerva

OCCUPATION Super-villain, former archaeologist

HEIGHT 5 ft 9 in (1.75 m)

WEIGHT 140 lb (64 kg)

BASE Mobile

MAIN ALLIES Legion of Doom, Secret Society of Super-Villains, Godwatch

MAIN FOES Wonder Woman, Urzkartaga, Dr. Veronica Cale

UNWILLING BRIDE

Barbara is tricked by Veronica Cale into joining a research expedition to Bwunda in Africa, where she is wedded against her will to the plant god Urzkartaga and transformed into the animalistic Cheetah. Before the trip, her friend Wonder Woman gives Barbara an emergency signal to summon her if she gets into trouble, but Cale disables it. Barbara blames Wonder Woman for abandoning her, and friends become enemies.

CHESHIRE
POISONOUS ASSASSIN

The assassin known as Cheshire is one of the world's deadliest. In addition to being an exceptional martial artist and acrobat, she also uses fake fingernails to administer deadly poisons to her targets. Despite her wicked, mercenary ways, Cheshire and the hero Arsenal seem to be drawn to each other.

VITAL STATS

REAL NAME Jade Nguyen

OCCUPATION Assassin

HEIGHT 5 ft 9 in (1.75 m)

WEIGHT 135 lb (61 kg)

BASE Mobile

MAIN ALLIES League of Assassins, Ninth Circle

MAIN FOES The Outlaws, Green Arrow

TOXIC RELATIONSHIP

When Cheshire arrives to help Arsenal defeat a group of Intergang thugs, Roy thinks his dangerous ex-girlfriend may be ready to use her skills for heroism. But sneaky Cheshire is just using it as an opportunity to get close to Roy in order to poison him!

POWERS

Cheshire is one of the most lethal martial artists in the world, skilled in many ancient fighting techniques forgotten by others. She is also an expert in toxins and often wears poisoned fingernails or wields poisoned weapons, with which she is a fearsome combatant.

A scratch from Cheshire's nails can deliver a deadly poison

Cheshire's costume is green to match her real name, Jade

CIRCE
ANCIENT WITCH

The deadly witch Circe has lived for centuries without aging. She once heard a prophecy saying that a daughter of Hippolyta will cause her downfall, so she sees Wonder Woman as an enemy. Although Circe has been known to make alliances, her total self-interest always leads her to betray her allies in the end.

Eyes are red with yellow pupils and sometimes flash with magical lightning

SAVING HER SOUL

When Circe loses her soul, she also loses her immortality. She fears death, so she attempts to use the Pandora Pits, pools of unimaginable evil, as a portal to the realm where her soul is held. Circe captures Superman, Wonder Woman, Deadman, and Zatanna, using their powers to increase her own and access the Pits. But Circe is defeated when Batman and the Outlaws arrive to free their friends.

Circe's beauty has lured many men into her clutches to become inhuman Ani-Men

VITAL STATS

REAL NAME Circe

OCCUPATION Witch

HEIGHT 5 ft 11 in (1.80 m)

WEIGHT 135 lb (61 kg)

BASE Aeaea

MAIN ALLIES Ani-Men, Rā's al Ghūl, Lex Luthor

MAIN FOES Wonder Woman, Hippolyta

POWERS

Circe is a powerful sorceress who can wield her magic to attack others and to protect herself. Her unique talent is creating Ani-Men. These are unfortunate humans turned into animals by a spell, which also forces them to obey Circe's every command.

CLAYFACE
REFORMED SHAPE-SHIFTER

Forever changed by exposure to a strange, claylike substance, Basil Karlo is the monstrous Clayface. He starts out using his incredible shape-shifting powers for crime but eventually tires of this life and agrees to reform. Clayface joins The Gotham Knights team of heroes formed by Batman.

Clayface's strength increases as he grows larger

VITAL STATS

REAL NAME Basil Karlo

OCCUPATION Actor

HEIGHT Various

WEIGHT Various

BASE Gotham City

MAIN ALLIES The Gotham Knights

MAIN FOES Victim Syndicate, formerly Batman

Clayface can shape his limbs into weapons

RAMPAGING KNIGHT

When Clayface is trapped by the Victim Syndicate, its members remove the inhibitor bracelet that stops him from losing control and becoming a monster. Clayface starts rampaging through the streets of Gotham City. His Gotham Knights teammates try to help him but cannot save him. Batwoman shoots him to prevent further casualties.

POWERS

Clayface can alter his shape into any form or size, including animals and other humans. When he takes on the shape of a person, the changes are not just on the surface but right down to the DNA. This means that if he changes to imitate a being with powers, he can also use their powers while mimicking their shape.

COMMISSIONER JIM GORDON
PROTECTING AND SERVING GOTHAM CITY

Commissioner James "Jim" Gordon is an honest cop trying to protect Gotham City from crime. He is Batman's link to the authorities, consulting with the Dark Knight on police investigations. Gordon also allows Batman to operate even though he is an outlawed vigilante. Jim is also the father of Barbara Gordon, a.k.a. Batgirl, and has even taken on a heroic identity himself for a time.

Gordon uses every weapon he can to keep Gotham City safe

VITAL STATS

REAL NAME James "Jim" Gordon

OCCUPATION Police Commissioner

HEIGHT 5 ft 9 in (1.75 m)

WEIGHT 168 lb (76 kg)

BASE Gotham City

MAIN ALLIES Batman

MAIN FOES The Joker

Glasses and a neatly trimmed mustache are Gordon's signature look

BATMAN 2.0

When Batman is believed to have died, Gotham City needs a new Dark Knight. Gordon dons the Batsuit, albeit a more mechanized one than the previous Batman. Although declaring it to be "the dumbest idea in the history of Gotham City," Gordon heroically protects the city as Batman. He stands down when Bruce Wayne returns to reclaim the cowl.

POWERS

As a former marine, Jim Gordon is trained in hand-to-hand combat and other military skills, including marksmanship. He is also an expert in criminal investigations. His strong moral values are what lead Batman to place his trust in Gordon despite the corruption of many other police officers in Gotham City.

CRIME SYNDICATE
THE EVIL JUSTICE LEAGUE

Evil is the natural order of things on the alternate-universe world of Earth-3. Here, instead of a Justice League, there is the Crime Syndicate—a twisted team of super-villains who decide to stage an invasion of Prime Earth. Although the villains seem to have defeated the Justice League, they do not capture Batman. This error leads to their own downfall.

RECRUITS FOR EVIL

The Crime Syndicate recruits most of Prime Earth's super-villains into a Secret Society to support its invasion. However, not all the villains like the Crime Syndicate's plans for Prime Earth, and some actually help Batman rescue the trapped Justice League.

MEMBERS INCLUDE

Each member of the Crime Syndicate is an evil version of an Earth hero.

1. **OWLMAN**—Batman
2. **DEATHSTORM**—Firestorm
3. **JOHNNY QUICK**—The Flash
4. **POWER RING**—Green Lantern
5. **ULTRAMAN**—Superman
6. **SUPERWOMAN**—Wonder Woman

CYBORG
CYBERNETIC SUPERSTAR

Victor Stone becomes Cyborg after being wounded in an explosion at S.T.A.R. Labs. In the top-secret Red Room, his father Dr. Silas Stone saves Victor's life by replacing his broken body parts with artificial components. Victor joins the Justice League as Cyborg, bringing incredible powers to the team thanks to his cutting-edge technology.

Cybory can transform this arm into a powerful sonic cannon

Eye has many functions, including telescopic and X-ray vision

Hands are made from strong metal

VITAL STATS

REAL NAME Victor "Vic" Stone

OCCUPATION Super Hero

HEIGHT 6 ft 6 in (1.98 m)

WEIGHT 385 lb (175 kg)

BASE Justice League Watchtower

MAIN ALLIES Justice League, S.T.A.R. Labs, Metal Men

MAIN FOES Grid, Darkseid

DEFEATING DARKSEID

While still struggling to understand his new powers, Cyborg is transported via a portal to where the Justice League is about to face Darkseid. Victor's technology lets him access information from the powerful Mother Boxes and find a way to defeat the super-villain. After the Super Heroes' victory, Cyborg is welcomed as the League's newest member.

POWERS

Cyborg's advanced technology gives him a huge range of powers, including a super-strong body that can produce powerful weaponry and useful tools. He can create portals, named Boom Tubes, that can teleport him anywhere. Cyborg's powers are continually increasing as he upgrades himself.

CYBORG SUPERMAN
GHOST IN THE MACHINE

Astronaut Hank Henshaw loses his family and his body following an accident in space. But Hank's mind survives, and he gains the ability to transfer it into machines. Hank blames Superman for failing to save his family, so he transfers himself into a cloned cybernetic version of the hero and plots his revenge as the Cyborg Superman.

POWERS

In his Cyborg Superman body, Hank has all the powers of the original Kryptonian, including super-strength, speed, stamina, and durability, plus flight, heat and X-ray vision, super-breath, and enhanced senses. He can also transfer his essence in an energy form to any other machine.

IMPRISONED IN THE PHANTOM ZONE

Cyborg Superman assembles the Superman Revenge Squad by gathering some of the Man of Steel's most dangerous foes, including General Zod and Mongul. The Squad nearly defeats the Superman Family, but the Man of Steel emerges victorious. After the defeat of the Squad, Superman imprisons Hank in the prison dimension known as the Phantom Zone for his crimes.

Cyborg Superman's obsession with the Man of Steel manifests itself in his appearance

VITAL STATS

REAL NAME Henry "Hank" Henshaw

OCCUPATION Super-villain

HEIGHT 6 ft 3 in (1.91 m)

WEIGHT 500 lb (227 kg)

BASE Phantom Zone

MAIN ALLIES Superman Revenge Squad

MAIN FOES Superman, Supergirl

DAMAGE
WEAPON OF MASS DESTRUCTION

Ethan Avery wants to serve his country, but he is turned into a monster—Damage. The US Army wants to use Damage as the ultimate weapon, going into situations no other soldier could. One problem is that Ethan can only become Damage for short periods of time. Another is that he is barely controllable as Damage, leaving a trail of destruction in his wake.

POWERS

Damage possesses almost limitless levels of superhuman strength, as well as extreme durability against attacks. He is also able to leap long distances. However, Ethan can only maintain his powers for one hour, after which he returns to being an ordinary man. Ethan needs a 24-hour recovery period before he can become Damage again.

The Damage serum causes Ethan's skin to turn gray and his body to increase greatly in size and muscle mass

DAMAGE CONTROL

Amanda Waller sends her Task Force XI after Damage, in the hope of recruiting him to the team. However, her plan falls apart when Damage easily dispatches even this beefed-up Suicide Squad lineup, including Giganta, Solomon Grundy, and Parasite. When Wonder Woman arrives, she uses her lasso to show Damage the truth about the destruction he causes. Ethan is distraught and runs away.

Only Ethan's shorts usually survive the transformation into Damage

VITAL STATS

REAL NAME Ethan "Elvis" Avery

OCCUPATION Soldier

HEIGHT Variable

WEIGHT Variable

BASE Mobile

MAIN ALLIES Poison Ivy, Swamp Thing

MAIN FOES Colonel Marie Jonas, Gorilla Grodd

DARKSEID
RULER OF APOKOLIPS

Darkseid is one of the most powerful beings in the universe and one of the greatest threats to Earth and the Justice League. He is the ruler of Apokolips, a hellish planet of industrial wastelands and fire pits. Darkseid's leadership is brutal, and he is aided by his ruthless right-hand man, Desaad, and an army of evil Parademons.

Eyes can fire powerful Omega Beams

Skin takes on a rocky appearance after Darkseid takes the Omega Force into himself

POWERS

Darkseid is a being with incredible strength and intellect. His most powerful weapons are his Omega Beams, usually fired from his eyes. The Omega Beams are a form of cosmic energy that Darkseid can fire at any angle, or around corners, to hit his unfortunate victim. Darkseid can also use Mother Box technology to generate Boom Tubes, which he uses to travel across the universe.

BABY DARKSEID

Darkseid is apparently killed during a battle with the Anti-Monitor, his own daughter Grail, and the Justice League. But Grail uses an ancient Amazonian ritual to bring him back from the dead—in the form of a baby. Grail takes the baby Darkseid away to raise him in secret, waiting for his power to return to its previous level.

VITAL STATS

REAL NAME Uxas

OCCUPATION Intergalactic tyrant

HEIGHT 8 ft 9 in (2.67 m)

WEIGHT 1,815 lb (823 kg)

BASE Apokolips

MAIN ALLIES Desaad, Female Furies, Parademons

MAIN FOES Justice League, New Gods

DEADMAN
GHOST HERO

Former circus acrobat Boston Brand doesn't let a little thing like death stop him from helping people. He used to be a trapeze artist performing under the stage name Deadman, which he keeps as a code name in his afterlife. To make up for the sins of his life, Deadman possesses living people in order to try to make their lives better. He is a member of the supernatural team Justice League Dark.

HAUNTED HOUSE

Deadman is used to helping the living, but when he gets trapped in a haunted house, he needs help from a young woman named Berenice. The two have to solve a 150-year-old murder mystery to allow Deadman to leave the place. Once the murder has been solved, Deadman says goodbye to Berenice and returns to his mission of helping people.

Deadman's creepy face is due to stage makeup he wore in life

As a ghost, Deadman wears the circus outfit he used to perform in

VITAL STATS

REAL NAME Boston Brand

OCCUPATION Super Hero

HEIGHT 6 ft (1.83 m)

WEIGHT Weightless

BASE Gotham City

MAIN ALLIES Justice League Dark, Batman

MAIN FOES Rama Kushna, Neron, Sensei

POWERS

As a ghost, Deadman is intangible and can move through solid objects. He is not bound by gravity like living people, so he can fly. Deadman is also invisible to most people, although those sensitive to the supernatural can see him. He can even possess living bodies, although he finds some can resist him.

DEADSHOT
THE MAN WHO NEVER MISSES

Floyd Lawton goes by the code name Deadshot because he is one of the world's greatest marksmen. Making his living as a hired gun, Deadshot ends up in prison, and from there is recruited to join Amanda Waller's Suicide Squad. His utter dedication to the mission at hand is only equalled by his complete disregard for his own safety.

The red eye on Deadshot's suit is a targeting device to give his shots added precision

Deadshot's armored suit gives extra protection against his many enemies

UNLIKELY TEAM-UP

Deadshot is surprised when his former enemy Batman breaks him out of Belle Reve Penitentiary. Deadshot's daughter, Zoe, has been kidnapped, and the Dark Knight wants the villain's help to find her. However, Batman refuses to let Deadshot use his normally lethal methods. The two come to blows, and Batman tells Deadshot that he can't be a bad guy now that he is a father.

POWERS

Deadshot's skill with guns is so advanced that it is almost a superpower. He is one of the world's deadliest assassins and is willing to put himself at considerable personal risk in order to fulfill a contract. He is also a skilled mechanical engineer and constructed his signature wrist-mounted machine guns himself.

VITAL STATS

REAL NAME Floyd Lawton

OCCUPATION Assassin

HEIGHT 6 ft 1 in (1.85 m)

WEIGHT 202 lb (92 kg)

BASE Belle Reve Penitentiary

MAIN ALLIES Suicide Squad

MAIN FOES Batman, Kobra Cult

DEATHSTROKE
WORLD'S DEADLIEST ASSASSIN

Deathstroke is widely feared as the world's most lethal assassin. He feels that what he does is just a job—one he can do better than anyone else. As a highly decorated former soldier, he is not one to question orders, or the morality of the tasks he is given. Eventually, however, he comes to question the ethics of his work and tries to find ways to make it right.

VITAL STATS

REAL NAME Slade Wilson
OCCUPATION Mercenary, assassin
HEIGHT 6 ft 4 in (1.93 m)
WEIGHT 225 lb (102 kg)
BASE Mobile
MAIN ALLIES Hosun, Defiance
MAIN FOES Titans, Teen Titans, Cyborg, Batman

Deathstroke wears the Ikon suit, which absorbs the energy of attacks to protect the wearer

Deathstroke's mask needs only a single eye hole, as he is blind in his right eye

DEFIANCE

Deathstroke decides to give up being an assassin and become a force for good. When nobody believes him, he forms a super-team called Defiance. Other members include Kid Flash and Power Girl, plus his children Rose and Jericho. Although the team does not last, Deathstroke tries not to return to his former life.

POWERS

Deathstroke's formidable skills are enhanced by an experimental serum. He has advanced mental capacity, accelerated healing, super-strength and durability, and heightened reflexes. He is extremely skilled in multiple martial arts and with a wide variety of weapons. Deathstroke also has a very slow aging process and resistance to toxins.

THE DEMON
RELUCTANT HERO

Etrigan the Demon is bound to the upstanding human Jason Blood by a powerful spell, cast by the wizard Merlin. The demon loves combat, and Blood speaks an ancient rhyme whenever he needs Etrigan to take over for him in battle. While Etrigan is in control, Blood exists on Earth only in intangible form.

POWERS

Etrigan is incredibly strong and durable, with accelerated healing. He can blast fire at his enemies or use his demonic teeth or claws when fighting at close quarters. Although able to face most metahumans in combat, he is vulnerable to magic. He also weakens the longer that he stays on Earth and recharges by returning to Hell.

VITAL STATS

REAL NAME Etrigan

OCCUPATION Demon

HEIGHT 6 ft 4 in (1.93 m)

WEIGHT 3,512 lb (1,593 kg)

BASE Hell

MAIN ALLIES Jason Blood, Demon Knights, Madame Xanadu

MAIN FOES Morgaine Le Fey, Merlin, Belial

When Etrigan is enjoying himself, he speaks in rhyme

KING OF HELL

When his father Belial tries to invade Earth with the armies of Hell, Etrigan senses an opportunity. Etrigan helps his host Jason fight off the danger to Earth, hoping he might be able to overthrow his father and become King of Hell. Etrigan wins the day—and the throne—with the help of the wizard Merlin and the legendary sword Excalibur.

DESPERO

EVIL ALIEN TELEPATH

Despero is an alien tyrant from the planet Kalanor. He wants to conquer many worlds, but is particularly drawn to Earth because he would relish the challenge of defeating its metahuman protectors. While he has been captured by Earth's defenders more than once, it is difficult finding a prison that will hold the mighty extraterrestrial.

POWERS

Despero has superhuman strength and durability, but he also has incredible psychic powers, which were given to him by the magical source of power called the Flame of Py'tar. He can read and control the minds of others, as well as using his own mind to move objects. He also has a genius-level intellect.

Red skin and a webbed fin on the head are typical for a Kalanorian

BATTLE OF THE TELEPATHS

When Despero breaks out of prison and attacks the Justice League's base, only inexperienced heroes— Element Woman, Firestorm, and the Atom—are at home. They are saved by the arrival of Martian Manhunter, who engages Despero in a battle that is partly physical and partly conducted in their minds. Martian Manhunter wins the day by using his powers at full strength, leaving Despero in a heap on the floor.

VITAL STATS

REAL NAME Despero

OCCUPATION World conqueror

HEIGHT 8 ft 1 in (2.46 m)

WEIGHT 850 lb (386 kg)

BASE Kalanor

MAIN ALLIES Secret Society of Super-Villains, Crime Syndicate

MAIN FOES Justice League, Martian Manhunter

DETECTIVE CHIMP
SIMIAN INVESTIGATOR

Bobo is a cruelly treated circus chimpanzee who manages to escape captivity and ends up drinking from the Fountain of Youth. The fountain's water gives him super-intelligence and the ability to talk to any other creature. Bobo puts these skills to use as Detective Chimp, an old-school private investigator.

POWERS

Detective Chimp's most amazing superpower is that he can talk to any species of animal, including humans. His outstanding intelligence makes him one of the world's greatest detectives.

Bobo wears an old friend's hat, which happens to be a deerstalker just like Sherlock Holmes's

HIDDEN HEROES

With the Multiverse under threat from the demon Barbatos, Detective Chimp tries to help the Science Squad figure out solutions. Bobo, however, can feel his intelligence "de-evolving," and all hope seems lost for him. Luckily, he is contacted by a team of primate heroes from the previously unknown world of Earth-53, who have come to save his mind and fight Barbatos.

VITAL STATS

REAL NAME Bobo T. Chimpanzee

OCCUPATION Private investigator

HEIGHT 3 ft 7 in (1.09 m)

WEIGHT 76 lb (34 kg)

BASE Los Angeles, California

MAIN ALLIES Justice League Dark, Science Squad

MAIN FOES None

Since becoming super-intelligent, Bobo has worn clothes to appear more professional

DOCTOR FATE
MIGHTY SORCERER

Doctor Fate is a powerful sorcerer whose possession of certain magical artifacts gives him almost unstoppable mystic abilities. Formerly an archaeologist named Kent Nelson, Doctor Fate is a Super Hero who faces the worst supernatural threats to Earth and beyond. Doctor Fate is happy to team up with a variety of other Super Heroes and teams when the need arises.

The Helmet of Anubis is one of the most powerful objects in the universe

POWERS

Doctor Fate possesses various magical artifacts—including the Helmet of Anubis, the Cloak of Destiny, and the Amulet of Anubis. These items give him the power of flight, teleportation, and spellcasting, among many other extraordinary magical abilities. He is also nearly invulnerable and immortal.

FATE TO THE RESCUE

Earth's heroes are cornered by the Dark Knights—twisted, villainous versions of Batman from the Dark Multiverse. Fortunately, Doctor Fate teleports the heroes to the Oblivion Bar, a safe place in a magic pocket dimension. Here, Fate, Steel, and Mister Terrific figure out how the Nth Metal, including that in Fate's helmet, may be the key to defeating the Dark Multiverse.

VITAL STATS

REAL NAME Kent Nelson

OCCUPATION Sorcerer, former archaeologist

HEIGHT 6 ft 2 in (1.88 m)

WEIGHT 197 lb (89 kg)

BASE Salem, Massachusetts

MAIN ALLIES Justice League Dark, Justice Society of America

MAIN FOES Barbatos, Black Adam

DOCTOR LIGHT
DAZZLING VILLAIN

Arthur Light is a scientist at a secret government facility when a lab accident kills him. He manages to live on as a consciousness made of pure light. Originally a good man, Light's rage at the loss of his life causes him to seek revenge against the government agencies whom he believes allowed it to happen.

Doctor Light's appearance is an illusion made from light, but he creates himself a costume worthy of a super-villain

VITAL STATS

REAL NAME Arthur Light

OCCUPATION Super-villain

HEIGHT 5 ft 11 in (1.80 m)

WEIGHT 171 lb (78 kg)

BASE Chetlan United Atlantic Islands

MAIN ALLIES The Crimson Men, Deathstroke, Secret Society of Super-Villains

MAIN FOES A.R.G.U.S.

POWERS

Doctor Light can absorb the light around him, which can then be released in dazzling, explosive blasts. He can also control and form light at will. His intelligence enables him to create hard-light constructs in humanoid form that act as his army.

LIGHT REFRESHMENTS

When he loses his family, Light abandons his villainous ways and lives on a remote island. Light's old comrade Deathstroke visits him, and they catch up over a coffee. Deathstroke points out that Light is walking through a table, so Light tells him that he is no longer alive but is made of light. After his friend leaves, Light wistfully recalls his old life as a villain.

DOCTOR MID-NITE

SUPER HERO SURGEON

As a baby, Pieter Cross is delivered by the original Doctor Mid-Nite, Charles McNider. Cross becomes a doctor in adulthood but is blinded during an accident involving a mysterious new drug. The incident also gives him superpowers, which he uses to fight crime as the new Doctor Mid-Nite. Cross still frequently uses his medical skills on injured teammates.

Doctor Mid-Nite's trained owl is named Charlie, after the original Doctor Mid-Nite

Doctor Mid-Nite's infrared lenses can let him "see" in daylight

POWERS

Doctor Mid-Nite is able to see only in pitch darkness, in which case his vision is enhanced to superhuman levels. He invents blackout bombs to hinder his opponents and give him the upper hand even in daytime fights. Doctor Mid-Nite is also a skilled physician.

A TERRIBLE GIFT

When the powerful being Gog comes to Earth, he gives gifts to some heroes, including restoring Doctor Mid-Nite's sight. This blessing, however, is not all it seems. Doctor Mid-Nite's blackout bombs are now useless to him, and the loss of infrared vision means he is unable to assess medical conditions as well as before. This makes him unable to operate on critically wounded Justice Society ally Lance.

VITAL STATS

REAL NAME Pieter Cross

OCCUPATION Doctor, Super Hero

HEIGHT 5 ft 10 in (1.78 m)

WEIGHT 175 lb (79 kg)

BASE Portsmouth City, Oregon

MAIN ALLIES Justice Society of America

MAIN FOES Doctor Light, Terrible Trio, Ultra-Humanite

DOCTOR POISON
TOXIC ENEMY

Colonel Marina Maru is Doctor Poison, a mercenary and poison expert working for a shady organization called Godwatch. Doctor Poison works out of the sub-basement of Empire Enterprises, which is owned by Veronica Cale—a businesswoman and Godwatch's leader. Poison's job is to help Cale find Wonder Woman, and then the location of Themyscira.

Doctor Poison's mask conceals her identity

VITAL STATS

REAL NAME Marina Maru

OCCUPATION Scientist, mercenary

HEIGHT 5 ft 4 in (1.63 m)

WEIGHT 119 lb (54 kg)

BASE Empire Enterprises, Washington, D.C.

MAIN ALLIES Godwatch, Team Poison

MAIN FOES Wonder Woman

POWERS

Doctor Poison, as her name suggests, is an expert in the manufacture and use of poisons and toxins. She creates a chemical named the Maru Virus, which turns people into relentless killers. She is also a highly trained member of the military.

HARD TARGET

Doctor Poison and her team are given Wonder Woman as a target. She sends her group after Steve Trevor to distract Wonder Woman. Poison herself sits on a rooftop waiting for the chance to shoot the hero. Although she does in fact shoot Wonder Woman twice, the hero still has the strength to spring up to Doctor Poison's vantage point and defeat her.

DOCTOR SIVANA

SEEKER OF MAGIC

Doctor Thaddeus Sivana devotes his life to studying magic after science fails to save his family from a horrible threat. In search of a mystical solution, Sivana discovers the long-lost tomb of the magical villain Black Adam. Sivana releases the villain back into the world, but his own body is changed by his exposure to magic.

Doctor Sivana has a lightning-shaped scar on his face that he got when opening the tomb of Black Adam

VITAL STATS

REAL NAME Thaddeus Sivana
OCCUPATION Scientist
HEIGHT 5 ft 6 in (1.68 m)
WEIGHT 123 lb (56 kg)
BASE Blackhawk Island
MAIN ALLIES Science Squad, Black Adam
MAIN FOES The Shazam Family

POWERS

Doctor Sivana is a scientist with a genius-level intellect, although since being struck by lightning his sanity is questionable. Sivana can see magic since one of his eyes is connected to the magical world. However, using magic causes him physical pain.

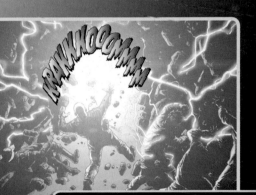

FINDING ADAM

Doctor Sivana travels to the Iraqi Desert in search of Black Adam's tomb. As he tries to break it open, he is struck by magic lightning, giving him the ability to see magic. He reads aloud the magic lettering "Shazam!" on the tomb and frees Black Adam. The newly freed villain discovers that Sivana speaks his language and uses him as an assistant.

DONNA TROY
WONDER GIRL

Donna Troy is created from clay by a sorceress, who wants to use her as a weapon to hurt Wonder Woman. However, the plot is foiled, and Donna is brought to Themyscira, where she is raised as an Amazonian warrior. Later coming to "Man's World," she joins the Teen Titans and eventually becomes a Titans member.

Donna's bracelets enable her to deflect bullets

Donna often wields a sword and shield in battle

FUTURE IMPERFECT

Donna gets a big shock when she realizes that the mysterious figure who has been plotting against the Titans is ... a future version of herself. This incarnation, named Troia, travels back in time to tell Donna she doesn't need the Titans and that she will become a world conqueror. Donna rejects the idea that her future is already written and defeats Troia in battle.

POWERS

Donna Troy is an expert warrior who has been trained by the Amazons. She has the same powers as a true Amazon—super-strength, speed, durability, and flight. She is immortal if she remains uninjured in battle. Donna's courage increases when she is defending one of her friends.

VITAL STATS

REAL NAME Donna Troy

OCCUPATION Super Hero

HEIGHT 5 ft 9 in (1.75 m)

WEIGHT 135 lb (61 kg)

BASE Titans Tower, New York City

MAIN ALLIES Titans, the Amazons

MAIN FOES Mister Twister, H.I.V.E., Fearsome Five

DOOM PATROL
THE WORLD'S STRANGEST HEROES

The Doom Patrol was originally brought together by Dr. Niles Caulder, an unethical scientist who gave bizarre metahuman powers to its members against their will. Forced to leave their old lives behind, his chosen ones would fight evil as the Doom Patrol. The team eventually asks Caulder to leave after he interferes with their abilities one time too many.

MEMBERS INCLUDE

1. ROBOTMAN Clifford Steele's brain is now housed in a powerful robotic body.

2. JANE Jane has multiple personalities, each of which has its own superpower.

3. CASEY "SPACE CASE" BRINKE The sentient road named Danny the Street brought this comic book character to life.

4. FUGG This unusual creature can say only its name—Fugg—but has a tape player in its stomach.

5. FLEX MENTALLO This strongman Super Hero can alter reality by flexing his muscles.

6. NEGATIVE MAN Lawrence Trainor can leave his body as a being of pure energy.

MILK WARS

The Doom Patrol arrives in Happy Harbor, Rhode Island, to investigate an evil firm called Retconn. Its members find a version of the Justice League of America (JLA) works for Retconn, including an alternate Superman named Milkman Man. The city's inhabitants are kept in line with doctored milk, delivered by this dairy hero. When the Doom Patrol show the JLA their actual origins, the two teams join forces to stop Retconn.

DOOMSDAY
THE ULTIMATE SURVIVOR

Genetically engineered to survive Krypton's most inhospitable environments, Doomsday is a formidable creature. The circumstances of his creation have left him with a burning hatred for all Kryptonians, and he hunts them relentlessly. Doomsday even manages to kill Superman on one occasion, although the Man of Steel is resurrected.

POWERS

Doomsday is created in a lab in Krypton's harshest landscape. Sent out to die repeatedly in the hostile environment, he is cloned over and over again until he is able to evolve himself rapidly to counter any threat. His strength and durability make him almost unbeatable.

Although cloned from a humanoid, Doomsday's forced evolution has turned him into a monster

ZONING OUT

Doomsday is on the rampage on Earth and seemingly unstoppable, even with the combined might of Wonder Woman and Superman against him. But Superman has learned the hard way that in a fight with Doomsday, you must have a plan. Luring the monster to his Fortress of Solitude, Superman turns on his Phantom Zone Projector, and Doomsday is sucked into it.

Doomsday's skin releases a powerful toxin that causes anything near him to wither and die

VITAL STATS

REAL NAME None

OCCUPATION Hunter

HEIGHT 8 ft 10 in (2.69 m)

WEIGHT 915 lb (415 kg)

BASE Phantom Zone

MAIN ALLIES None

MAIN FOES Superman, Supergirl, Superboy

ECLIPSO
SPIRIT OF VENGEANCE

Eclipso is an evil entity that corrupts anything he comes into contact with. When Eclipso possesses someone, he unlocks their darkest thoughts and makes them act on them. Eclipso becomes trapped inside a diamond known as the Heart of Darkness, which is recorded as being present at some of the worst events in history.

ECLIPSO UNLEASHED

Villain Max Lord attempts to use the Heart of Darkness to mind-control everyone on Earth. He incorrectly thinks he is strong enough to control Eclipso, and the entity takes him over. Eclipso proceeds to make people do terrible things, and even controls most of the Suicide Squad and the Justice League. He makes the mistake of ignoring the teams' apparently less powerful members, Killer Frost and Batman, who in the end defeat him.

Half of Eclipso's face is blue, and the same markings appear on anyone he possesses

When Eclipso is free of the Heart of Darkness, he wears it on his chest

VITAL STATS

REAL NAME Kalaa

OCCUPATION Spirit of Vengeance

HEIGHT Variable

WEIGHT Variable

BASE Heart of Darkness

MAIN ALLIES Maxwell Lord

MAIN FOES Justice League, Suicide Squad

POWERS

Eclipso is a magical spirit with a wide range of extraordinary powers. When anyone touches his Heart of Darkness gem, he can force them to do whatever he wants. He is invulnerable to injury and immortal, but he can be trapped within the Heart of Darkness.

EL DIABLO
CURSED CRIMINAL

Chato Santana, a.k.a. El Diablo, is consumed with guilt after allowing his powers to harm innocent people. He lets himself be imprisoned in Belle Reve Penitentiary, where he is recruited into the Suicide Squad. El Diablo is happy he can atone for his crimes, and Task Force X gets his extraordinary pyrokinetic powers.

POWERS

El Diablo has total control over fire. Chato can create flames out of nothing and alter their temperature to whatever he needs it to be. His powers come from the curse of El Diablo, which also fills him with a desire for vengeance against others who have done wrong. It also makes El Diablo immortal.

When El Diablo is preparing for battle, his forearms appear surrounded by flames

Extensive tattoos are from his time as a gangster

HEAT SEEKING

El Diablo is on a mission near the US border with Mexico when he is challenged by a LexCorp robot. The machine fires missiles at him, and El Diablo quickly realizes that they are attracted to heat. El Diablo conjures up a trail of fire in the air, which the missiles follow away from him back toward the robot. The machine is destroyed in a massive explosion.

FWOOSH

VITAL STATS

REAL NAME Chato Santana

OCCUPATION Suicide Squad member

HEIGHT 6 ft (1.83 m)

WEIGHT 182 lb (83 kg)

BASE Belle Reve Penitentiary

MAIN ALLIES Suicide Squad

MAIN FOES Jake Dalesko

ELONGATED MAN
ELASTIC FANTASTIC

Ralph Dibny is Elongated Man, a hero with incredible stretching powers. He is also one of the best detectives in the world and is happily married to Sue Dibny. Although the two do not have children, they acquire a surrogate family in the form of the kooky super-team the Secret Six.

Elongated Man can stretch into many shapes, but not complex objects like vehicles

VITAL STATS

REAL NAME Ralph Dibny

OCCUPATION Private investigator

HEIGHT 6 ft 1 in (1.85 m)

WEIGHT 178 lb (81 kg)

BASE Central City

MAIN ALLIES Sue Dibny, Secret Six, The Flash (Barry Allen)

MAIN FOES League of Assassins, the Riddler, Doctor Light

POWERS

Elongated Man can stretch his body to extraordinary lengths and flatten it to get through small gaps. The more stretched he is, the harder it is for Elongated Man to control his power. Ralph cannot stretch himself into complicated forms, but he can change into simple shapes.

Elongated Man's suit can stretch with him

BOUNCING BACK

After his wife disappears, Elongated Man is delighted when she returns. He is reunited with his amazing abilities and his wife, Sue. Feeling refreshed, he leads the Secret Six on a mission to rescue one of their teammates from the League of Assassins. Ralph turns himself into a parachute shape to lower the team into position and then flattens himself to enter the supposedly impregnable building through a grille.

ENCHANTRESS
DEMONIC SORCERESS

The super-villain Enchantress is a powerful sorceress who is trapped within the innocent human June Moone. June can let Enchantress take control, but the villain sometimes forcibly takes over during stressful situations. As Enchantress, June wields awesome magical powers and does not care about collateral damage. This makes her an incredibly valuable, but highly dangerous, member of the Suicide Squad.

The Enchantress can summon magical energy in the form of green light

When Enchantress takes over June, she wears a green hooded costume

DEFEATING SUPERMAN

When the Suicide Squad are ordered to prevent the Justice League from capturing them alive, Enchantress finds herself facing the Man of Steel. She allows him to believe that he is reaching the June side of her persona, but it is a ploy. She hits Superman with a powerful magical blast, one of the few things he is vulnerable to, and knocks him out.

VITAL STATS

REAL NAME June Moone

OCCUPATION Graphic designer

HEIGHT 5 ft 6 in (1.68 m)

WEIGHT 126 lb (57 kg)

BASE Belle Reve Penitentiary

MAIN ALLIES Suicide Squad

MAIN FOES Justice League Dark, The Wall

POWERS

Enchantress has a phenomenal range of magical powers. She can fire energy blasts, fly, and transform objects. She also possesses many psychic powers, including manipulating the emotions of others, telekinesis, and the ability to manipulate reality itself. Her demonic tendencies mean that she will use her powers for evil if she ever escapes Amanda Waller's strict control.

ETTA CANDY
WONDER WOMAN'S BEST FRIEND

When Wonder Woman arrives in "Man's World," her first female friend is Etta Candy. They share a close and loyal bond, and Wonder Woman even promises to move in with an injured Etta to act as nurse and housekeeper. Etta is also a good friend of Steve Trevor, having served with him at A.R.G.U.S. for many years.

Etta is very tough, and opponents underestimate her at their peril

POWERS

Etta Candy has no superpowers but is trained by the US Navy. She is brave and skilled with firearms and in hand-to-hand combat. Etta's leadership qualities are recognized when she is promoted to the rank of commander by A.R.G.U.S.

FIT FOR SERVICE

Despite being on medical leave due to an injury from a bomb attack, Etta rushes to defend her friend Wonder Woman when the Amazon is targeted by assassins. She courageously joins the fight, even attacking one of the assassins with her walking stick. Between Etta and Wonder Woman, all the attackers are defeated.

VITAL STATS

REAL NAME Etta Candy

OCCUPATION Businesswoman, Super Hero

HEIGHT 5 ft 3 in (1.60 m)

WEIGHT 135 lb (61 kg)

BASE Washington, D.C.

MAIN ALLIES Wonder Woman, Steve Trevor, A.R.G.U.S.

MAIN FOES Godwatch

FEARSOME FIVE
QUINTET OF CRIME

The Fearsome Five are the enemies of the Titans team, but they have also fought the Justice League—unsuccessfully. The brains of the team is the powerful telepath Psimon, although intellectual prowess also comes from Gizmo. The team is completed by "probability magician" Jinx and superpowered siblings Mammoth and Shimmer.

GOING STRAIGHT?

The Titans are suspicious when the Fearsome Five claim to have given up their abilities in an attempt to lead better lives. Sure enough, the Five are tricking people with metahuman abilities to give up their powers, so they can sell them. The villains even manage to get the better of the Titans in a fight until new Titan Bumblebee arrives.

MEMBERS INCLUDE

1. JINX This criminal has the power to give bad luck.

2. PSIMON Powerful Psimon has psychic abilities.

3. MAMMOTH This super-strong villain isn't that smart.

4. SHIMMER Mammoth's sister can transmute materials.

5. GIZMO Smart Gizmo builds deadly gadgets.

FEMALE FURIES
WARRIORS OF APOKOLIPS

The Female Furies are Darkseid's elite warriors. They are led by Granny Goodness, who subjects her soldiers to a brutal training regime designed to weed out the weak. The Furies are fanatically loyal to Darkseid but often fight among themselves. If a member leaves the Furies, the rest of the group hunts them down. This includes their sometimes leader, sometimes adversary, Big Barda.

MEMBERS INCLUDE

1. STOMPA Menacing Stompa is the strongest Female Fury.

2. LASHINA This Fury wields electrical whips in battle.

3. BERNADETH Vicious Bernadeth uses the lethal Fahren-Knife, a gift from her brother, Desaad.

4. MAD HARRIET This villain fights with viciously sharp energy claws.

LOIS THE FURY

When Lois Lane-Kent is stranded on Apokolips, she is captured by the Female Furies, who dismiss her as "vermin." Lois soon earns their respect in a battle against an Apokoliptian Dredge Worm, however, and Granny Goodness makes her a Female Fury. Later, Lois turns against the Furies and helps Superman capture them.

FIRESTORM
NUCLEAR HERO

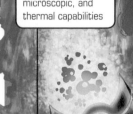

When Jason Rusch is caught in an explosion with fellow high-school student Ronnie Raymond, the two are fused together to make the metahuman Firestorm. Ronnie and Jason use the Firestorm Matrix to fuel their incredible powers, although not always harmoniously. Jason is the brains of the outfit, providing advice and wisdom, while class jock Ronnie takes care of the more physical side of missions.

Firestorm's eyes have enhanced vision, with X-ray, microscopic, and thermal capabilities

VITAL STATS

REAL NAME Jason Rusch and Ronnie Raymond

OCCUPATION Super Hero

HEIGHT 5 ft 8 in (1.73 m); 6 ft 1 in (1.85 m)

WEIGHT 150 lb (68 kg); 179 lb (81 kg)

BASE Walton Mills, Pennsylvania

MAIN ALLIES Martin Stein, Justice League

MAIN FOES Killer Frost

Firestorm's fire energy emanates from his body

THE JUSTICE LEAGUE'S PRISON

When the villainous Crime Syndicate of Earth-3 invades Prime Earth, Firestorm engages an evil incarnation of himself—named Deathstorm. The battle opens up the Firestorm Matrix inside the hero, which swallows up most of the Justice League. The Syndicate then imprisons Firestorm, who is becoming unstable. The heroes and villains opposing the Syndicate realize that they have to stop Firestorm going nuclear. Using Wonder Woman's lasso, they pull the heroes free of Firestorm, which cools him down.

POWERS

Firestorm is incredibly powerful, able to fly and fire energy blasts from his hands. He is super-strong and can even rearrange solid objects at the molecular level. However, the radiation held within Firestorm makes him very dangerous—if he overloads, he could cause a nuclear explosion.

THE FLASH (BARRY ALLEN)
THE FASTEST MAN ALIVE

Following a lightning strike in his laboratory, Barry Allen is connected to the Speed Force and given superpowers. He uses his new abilities to fight crime as The Flash. Barry is a big-hearted Super Hero who always wants to believe the best in everyone and is one of the founding members of the Justice League.

The Flash's earpieces are headphones, and he uses them to listen to police band radio

POWERS

The Flash's connection to the Speed Force gives him super-speed, reflexes, and stamina. He can vibrate the molecules in his body so fast that objects like bullets pass right through without harming him. The Flash can even travel in time if he uses his super-speed on the Cosmic Treadmill.

The Flash's costume accents match his Speed Force lightning

NEGATIVE FLASH

After being taken into the Negative Speed Force by Reverse-Flash, Barry Allen becomes Negative Flash. Now, black speed lightning crackles around Barry, and he is more aggressive than before. Barry is trying to learn how to control the Negative Speed Force with the help of Kid Flash, but then the new powers are forcibly removed by rogue speedster Fast Track.

The Flash's Speed Force lightning manifests in yellow

VITAL STATS

REAL NAME Bartholomew Henry "Barry" Allen

OCCUPATION Forensic investigator, Super Hero

HEIGHT 6 ft (1.83 m)

WEIGHT 195 lb (88 kg)

BASE Central City

MAIN ALLIES Justice League, the Flash Family

MAIN FOES Reverse-Flash, The Rogues, Gorilla Grodd

THE FLASH (WALLY WEST)
THE FLASH 2.0

Wally West is given Speed Force powers through an accident involving chemicals and a lightning strike. At first known as Kid Flash, Wally later becomes trapped in the Speed Force, and his very existence is erased from history. However, he manages to contact The Flash, a.k.a. Barry Allen, who remembers him and frees him. Now Barry and Wally both use The Flash code name.

Wally West's version of The Flash costume has a partial cowl, allowing his hair to be visible

Wally's costume is decorated with white lightning, the color of his lightning power since being trapped in the Speed Force

POWERS

As The Flash, Wally is connected to the Speed Force and has superhuman speed, reflexes, and stamina. He can also travel between dimensions and through time. Wally possesses accelerated healing and can also use the Speed Force to heal others. By vibrating the molecules of his body, Wally can become intangible and allow bullets to pass through him.

FLASH BACK

After escaping the Speed Force, Wally wants to reconnect with his best friends, the Titans. Unfortunately, they have forgotten him like everyone else. He breaks into Dick Grayson's apartment, but the Titans think he is an intruder and attack him. However, Wally realizes that a jolt of Speed Force energy will trigger the memories of his friends, and they share a joyful reunion.

VITAL STATS

REAL NAME Wallace Rudolph "Wally" West

OCCUPATION Super Hero

HEIGHT 6 ft (1.83 m)

WEIGHT 175 lb (79 kg)

BASE Keystone City; New York City

MAIN ALLIES Titans, The Flash (Barry Allen), Kid Flash

MAIN FOES Abra Kadabra, Zoom, Deathstroke

FREEDOM FIGHTERS
RESISTING THE OPPRESSOR

The Freedom Fighters are a patriotic Super Hero team based on Earth-X. In this reality, Superman's rocket lands in Germany. He becomes Overman and helps the Axis powers win World War II. After decades of harsh rule, the Freedom Fighters decide enough is enough. They band together and start making it clear to the authorities that they are going to bring liberty back to their country.

FREEDOM REVEALED

The Freedom Fighters choose their moment carefully to reveal their presence—the funeral of Overgirl, Overman's clone "daughter." Earth-X's evil Justice League captures a Freedom Fighter named the Human Bomb. The villains learn from him that the heroes have access to advanced weapons, training facilities, and a homemade superhuman program. And deep down, Overman is starting to think that the Freedom Fighters might have justice on their side ...

MEMBERS INCLUDE

BLACK CONDOR, DOLL MAN,
DOLL WOMAN, THE HUMAN BOMB,
PHANTOM LADY, THE RAY,
UNCLE SAM

GENERAL ZOD
KRYPTONIAN MENACE

General Zod is confined in a prison dimension called the Phantom Zone for his crimes against his planet Krypton. In this dimension, Zod survives the planet's destruction. He blames the House of El for his downfall. When he finds out that one of them—named Superman—has survived, Zod becomes the Man of Steel's mortal enemy.

Although almost invulnerable on Earth, Zod still wears Kryptonian battle armor

POWERS

When he comes to Earth, General Zod's powers are the same as Superman's—flight, super-strength, speed, stamina, and durability. He also has heat vision, X-ray vision, freeze breath, and super-breath. As a military commander, Zod is also skilled in combat and strategy.

Zod wears the symbol of the House of Zod

ZOD SQUAD

When the Suicide Squad inadvertently frees Zod from the Phantom Zone, Amanda Waller tries to recruit him to the team. She manages to put a Kryptonite brain bomb into his head, and Zod even goes on a mission with the Squad. But Zod does not want to take orders from a human, so he extracts his own brain bomb using his heat vision.

VITAL STATS

REAL NAME Dru-Zod

OCCUPATION General, super-villain

HEIGHT 6 ft 3 in (1.91 m)

WEIGHT 215 lb (98 kg)

BASE Phantom Zone

MAIN ALLIES Faora, Ursa, Lor-Zod

MAIN FOES Superman, Jor-El

GIGANTA
BIG AND BAD

Doris Zuel has a blood disease that inspires her to become a brilliant medical scientist. But the cure she creates for her illness also gives her the power to become a giant and fills her with rage. Giganta can cause a lot of damage at her massive size, and it takes someone with the strength of Wonder Woman to bring her down.

Giganta is very strong, even when normal-sized

Giganta's special costume grows with her

AGENT OF S.H.A.D.E.

Giganta is offered the chance to avoid jail if she works for S.H.A.D.E. (Super Human Advanced Defense Executive), an organization that combats threats from monsters. She finds that she is a natural at fighting strange or supernatural opponents and on one occasion takes down the brutal Vandal Savage using only her voice.

VITAL STATS

REAL NAME Doris Zuel

OCCUPATION Super-villain

HEIGHT 6 ft 6 in (1.98 m)

WEIGHT 220 lb (100 kg)

BASE Ivy Town

MAIN ALLIES Task Force XL, S.H.A.D.E.

MAIN FOES Wonder Woman

POWERS

Giganta can grow to a height of several hundred feet in a few seconds, with her strength and durability increasing as well. She can also use her voice as a sonic weapon while in giant size. However, it seems that growing to large sizes can also reduce her intelligence.

GOLDEN GLIDER
ASTRAL CRIMINAL

A former professional ice skater, Lisa Snart is caught up in the criminal ways of her brother Leonard, a.k.a. Captain Cold. When her physical body lies comatose in the hospital, Lisa gains the ability to use an intangible form. She takes the code name Golden Glider, becoming a career criminal and occasional leader of the Rogues.

In her astral form, Lisa is surrounded with a golden glow

Glider's ribbons are deadly weapons

A LOVING TOUCH

Golden Glider is dating Mirror Master, but he becomes trapped in an alternate dimension called Mirror World. Using her astral form, Lisa rescues him, but the strain is too much. Her astral form disappears, and her body nearly dies. Luckily, hospital staff treat her, and her astral body is later woken by the music of former Rogue Pied Piper.

VITAL STATS

REAL NAME Lisa Snart

OCCUPATION Criminal, former figure skater

HEIGHT 5 ft 5 in (1.65 m)

WEIGHT 117 lb (53 kg)

BASE Central City

MAIN ALLIES The Rogues

MAIN FOES The Flash (Barry Allen)

POWERS

When Golden Glider is in her astral form, she can go anywhere, fly, and move at very high speed. She can phase in and out of solid objects and surfaces. Lisa can also use ribbonlike tendrils to defeat an opponent without a trace.

GORILLA GRODD
INTELLIGENT APE

Gorilla Grodd is the leader of a super-intelligent race of apes, who, like The Flash (Barry Allen), derive their unusual abilities from the Speed Force. He despises humanity, especially Barry Allen, as he resents a pitiful human using the Speed Force. Grodd's enhanced psychic abilities and super-strength make him a formidable enemy.

Grodd's jaws are fearsomely strong, and unlike normal gorillas, he happily eats meat

POWERS

Thanks to his connection to the Speed Force, Grodd is super-intelligent and super-strong. He can also control and read minds. Grodd has a grim belief that he can gain the powers of others through eating their brains!

Grodd's body radiates Speed Force energy

GRODD CITY

When the Crime Syndicate from Earth-3 captures The Flash (Barry Allen), Central City is defenseless. Grodd travels there and disrupts peace talks between humans and gorillas. He makes the place his own, renaming it Grodd City. Grodd seems to have everything he has ever wanted, but he gets bored and returns to Gorilla City.

VITAL STATS

REAL NAME Grodd

OCCUPATION Megalomaniac

HEIGHT 6 ft 6 in (1.98 m)

WEIGHT 600 lb (272 kg)

BASE Central City; Gorilla City

MAIN ALLIES General Silverback, Poison Ivy

MAIN FOES The Flash (Barry Allen)

GREEN ARROW
EMERALD ARCHER

Oliver Queen is a billionaire businessman who wants to make a difference. Using his incredible skills with a bow and arrow, he takes to the streets as the masked hero Green Arrow, helping the poor and oppressed. Green Arrow is a member of the Justice League, and he alone has the power to destroy the League, if his teammates ever turn evil.

VITAL STATS

REAL NAME Oliver Queen

OCCUPATION Super Hero, businessman

HEIGHT 5 ft 10 in (1.85 m)

WEIGHT 176 lb (80 kg)

BASE Star City

MAIN ALLIES Justice League, Team Arrow, Black Canary

MAIN FOES Clock King, Ninth Circle, Dark Archer

Green Arrow wears a mask, and sometimes a hood, to conceal his identity

The quiver on Green Arrow's back stores all the arrows he needs for his missions

RUNAWAY TRAIN

Green Arrow, Black Canary, and their ally John Diggle are aboard for the maiden journey of the Empire Express, an underwater train between Shanghai and Seattle. A number of diplomats are also aboard, holding crucial peace talks. However, an assassin tries to stop the meeting and blows a hole in the underwater tunnel. With water rushing in, Diggle rescues the diplomats, while Green Arrow and Black Canary escape on a motorcycle.

POWERS

Green Arrow has no superpowers but is one of the world's best archers. He can use regular arrows as well as a range of "trick" arrows. Green Arrow is also an expert in martial arts and has highly developed survival skills.

GREEN LANTERN (GUY GARDNER)
POLICE THROUGH AND THROUGH

Guy Gardner is one of Earth's Green Lanterns. He is brash and reckless—but also brave, loyal, and fair. Guy was born into a family of Baltimore cops and has law enforcement in his DNA, so it is unsurprising that he becomes one of the most respected members of the Green Lantern Corps.

Guy's biker jacket is a unique, edgy take on the Green Lantern uniform

VITAL STATS

REAL NAME Guy Gardner

OCCUPATION Green Lantern, former police officer

HEIGHT 6 ft (1.83 m)

WEIGHT 180 lb (82 kg)

BASE Mogo

MAIN ALLIES Red Lanterns, Justice League International

MAIN FOES Xar, Guardians of the Universe

Power ring chose Guy while he was saving his brother from a gang

ONE ANGRY MAN

Guy is sent to infiltrate the Red Lantern Corps, whose power rings are fueled by rage. He defeats their leader in combat and assumes command, believing that the Red Lanterns can also be a force for good. His Green Lantern colleagues are unsure, but Guy negotiates the designation of their own space sector to patrol.

POWERS

With his Green Lantern power ring, Guy can create energy constructs using the force of his will. The ring also gives him the power of flight. Without it, he is a normal human, though one with unusually high levels of willpower and bravery.

GREEN LANTERN (HAL JORDAN)
THE MAVERICK LANTERN

Former test pilot Hal Jordan has a reputation for great courage ... and great recklessness. He is chosen as Earth's first member of the Green Lantern Corps. Now wielding a power ring, Hal travels through space fighting alien threats and is a key member of the Justice League.

Although Hal Jordan's identity is widely known, his mask is a signature part of his uniform

POWERS

Hal Jordan's power ring enables him to fly and create hard-light energy constructs. As a former pilot, Hal Jordan often creates airplane shapes. All Green Lanterns have extraordinary willpower, but Hal Jordan's is even stronger than most. After he loses his power ring, he forges another with his willpower alone.

Like all Green Lanterns, Jordan wears the symbol of the Corps on his suit

GREEN LANTERN VS. GENERAL ZOD

Kryptonian super-villain General Zod captures Jordan while he is without his power ring. The Green Lantern Corps mount a rescue mission, but it is going badly until Jordan manages to will his ring to return to him. With his power returned, Jordan attacks Zod with wave after wave of hard-light airplane constructs.

VITAL STATS

REAL NAME Hal Jordan

OCCUPATION Green Lantern

HEIGHT 6 ft 2 in (1.88 m)

WEIGHT 186 lb (84 kg)

BASE Mogo

MAIN ALLIES Green Lantern Corps, Justice League

MAIN FOES Sinestro, Parallax

GREEN LANTERN (JESSICA CRUZ)
CONQUERING FEAR

Jessica Cruz is terrified of leaving her apartment, but she is chosen by the evil Ring of Volthoom from Earth-3. The ring, which works through fear, enslaves Jessica until she is taught to control it by Batman and Hal Jordan. Eventually, Jessica joins the Green Lantern Corps. She is partnered with fellow Lantern Simon Baz to protect Earth's space sector.

Jessica's ring needs to be charged up at the same time as Simon Baz's

Jessica's right eye is surrounded by a Green Lantern symbol

SACRIFICE REWARDED

When The Flash (Barry Allen) is about to be killed by the evil Black Racer, Jessica hurls herself in between them. She saves Barry but is apparently killed. Fortunately, it is only the entity possessing her, Volthoom, who dies, and the evil power ring is destroyed. The Green Lantern Corps rewards her courage by choosing Jessica to be a real Green Lantern.

POWERS

Jessica has the usual powers given by a green power ring, including flight and the ability to create energy constructs. However, her relationship with her Green Lantern ring seems to be unique. The ring speaks and jokes with Jessica like a friend. Her past links to Volthoom and to her first evil ring enable her to access the other-dimensional Green Realm.

VITAL STATS

REAL NAME Jessica Cruz
OCCUPATION Green Lantern
HEIGHT 5 ft 6 in (1.68 m)
WEIGHT 137 lb (62 kg)
BASE Portland, Oregon
MAIN ALLIES Green Lantern Corps, Justice League
MAIN FOES Volthoom

GREEN LANTERN (JOHN STEWART)
LEADING BY EXAMPLE

Hailing from Detroit, Michigan, John Stewart is a US Marine and an architect before becoming a Green Lantern. Stewart serves with distinction in the Green Lantern Corps, rising to become its leader. His courage, tactical ability, and devotion to the Corps are vital components in his many battles against the universe's dark forces.

Stewart does not care about concealing his identity

VITAL STATS

REAL NAME John Stewart

OCCUPATION Green Lantern, former architect and US Marine

HEIGHT 6 ft 1 in (1.85 m)

WEIGHT 210 lb (91 kg)

BASE Mogo

MAIN ALLIES Indigo Tribe, Star Sapphire Corps

MAIN FOES Fatality, Alpha Lanterns, Durlans

LOST ARMY

The Green Lantern Corps is trapped in a dying universe, battling light-wielders who are draining its members' rings of their power. John rallies his teammates, urging them to go down fighting if they have to. He experiences flashbacks to his time in the US Marines and conjures a Marine unit made out of hard-light energy. When the Green Lanterns return to their own universe, John is their undisputed leader.

POWERS

John Stewart's power ring enables him to create green energy constructs using his willpower, as well as fly. Thanks to his military background, he is an excellent strategist and is proficient with firearms. He is also a born leader, making him the perfect choice to be commander of the Green Lantern Corps.

John Stewart's classic look is a mostly black costume with green details

GREEN LANTERN (KYLE RAYNER)
THE ART OF HEROISM

Artist Kyle Rayner is personally selected by one of the Guardians of the Universe to become a Green Lantern, while Hal Jordan is out of commission. Having proven himself as one of the most powerful and capable Green Lanterns, Kyle is appointed to the high rank of Honor Guard—elite Lanterns not restricted to a single space sector.

"Crab"-shaped mask is unique, created by Rayner to set himself apart from predecessor Hal Jordan

VITAL STATS

REAL NAME Kyle Rayner

OCCUPATION Green Lantern

HEIGHT 5 ft 11 in (1.80 m)

WEIGHT 180 lb (82 kg)

BASE Mogo

MAIN ALLIES Green Lantern Corps, Star Sapphire

MAIN FOES Guardians of the Universe, First Lantern

POWERS

Kyle Rayner's artistic talent is reflected in the light constructs he creates—more detailed and creative than any other Lantern's. Like other Lanterns, he can also use his power ring to fly and travel through space. While he is the White Lantern, Rayner also has healing powers.

WHITE LANTERN

Kyle Rayner is the only individual known to be able to wield all seven light colors of the emotional spectrum. When he masters this ability, he becomes the extremely powerful White Lantern, even able to bring Hal Jordan back to the realm of the living. However, Rayner has since returned to being a regular Green Lantern again.

White details on costume show Rayner's individuality as a Green Lantern and also reflect his time as the White Lantern

GREEN LANTERN (SIMON BAZ)
FROM CARS TO THE STARS

Former mechanic turned car thief Simon Baz is chosen as a Green Lantern by a unique power ring, fused from parts of rings previously worn by Hal Jordan and Sinestro. Baz finds it hard to have faith in himself, so he carries a gun in case he ever loses the ring. Eventually, Baz gains the confidence to leave his firearm behind.

Baz's ring originally creates a mask to conceal his identity when he is on the run

POWERS

Thanks to his power ring, Simon Baz can fly and form green energy constructs. Baz also has rare additional powers that Green Lanterns don't typically possess. His Emerald Sight enables him to see the near future. Baz can also use the force of his will to make his ring heal the wounded and sick.

Simon's tattoo means "courage" in Arabic

EMERALD SIGHT

The First Lantern Volthoom splinters Baz's first power ring into tiny fragments that become embedded in Baz's arm. The Green Lantern is rendered powerless, until he willfully forces the ring fragments to bring back his Emerald Sight. Baz can then see what the First Lantern is planning and is able to stop the villain.

Baz now wears one of the original seven green power rings

GREEN LANTERN CORPS
THE UNIVERSE'S POLICE FORCE

Members of the Green Lantern Corps are chosen for their exceptional willpower. Each Green Lantern is entrusted with the protection of sentient life and the delivery of justice in their designated space sector. The Guardians of the Universe founded the Green Lanterns and give them the Green Power Battery—the source of their light-wielding power.

MEMBERS INCLUDE

ARISIA RRAB, B'DG, GUY GARDNER, HAL JORDAN, JESSICA CRUZ, JOHN STEWART, KILOWOG, KYLE RAYNER, MOGO, SALAAK, SIMON BAZ, SORANIK NATU, TOMAR-TU

OA DESTROYED

The planet Oa had served as the home of the Green Lantern Corps for many millennia. However, even its powerful protectors could do nothing to prevent Oa from being destroyed by a being known as Relic. Following Oa's obliteration, the Green Lantern Corps uses Mogo—a sentient planet which is also a Green Lantern—as its base.

GUARDIAN
PROTECTOR OF THE PEOPLE

Guardian is a former US Air Force pilot and all-around good guy recruited by the Advanced Ideas Division of S.T.A.R. Labs. His name is Michael, but this might not be his birth name, and everything else about him is strictly classified. He is given a high-tech suit, an ultra-strong shield, and the task of being one of the protectors of Metropolis.

Guardian's armor is cutting-edge tech from S.T.A.R. Labs Advanced Ideas Division

POWERS

Guardian does not have superpowers but has a high-tech suit built by S.T.A.R. Labs to give him superhuman durability. His main weapon is his golden shield, which Guardian can also use as a hoverboard to travel around.

Guardian's golden shield provides a weapon, defensive capabilities, and even flight

SAVING SUPERBOY

When a deeply troubled Superboy shows up in Times Square, S.T.A.R. Labs dispatches Guardian to the scene. This Superboy appears to feed on superpowers so is disappointed that Guardian is "just" a human. He attacks Guardian, but the hero is able to easily fend off the attack. Guardian takes Superboy to S.T.A.R. Labs where the team discover that this is not the Superboy they know, but one from an alternate future.

VITAL STATS

REAL NAME Unknown

OCCUPATION Super Hero

HEIGHT 6 ft 1 in (1.85 m)

WEIGHT 205 lb (93 kg)

BASE Metropolis

MAIN ALLIES S.T.A.R. Labs, the Superman Family

MAIN FOES Parasite

HARLEY QUINN
THE QUEEN OF ZANY

Formerly a super-villain and sidekick to The Joker, Harley Quinn has moved on. While she may still be mischievous and zany, Harley has reformed and is now a Super Hero, who is a key member of the top-secret Suicide Squad. Harley lives on Coney Island and loyally protects her neighbors from harm.

POWERS

Harley's closeness with Poison Ivy led to her being granted a special immunity to toxins. She is a superb gymnast and weaves this skill into her unique fighting style. Harley is very brave and has shown leadership qualities from her time in the Suicide Squad.

VITAL STATS

REAL NAME Dr. Harleen Quinzel

OCCUPATION Psychiatrist, vigilante

HEIGHT 5 ft 7 in (1.70 m)

WEIGHT 115 lb (52 kg)

BASE Belle Reve Penitentiary; Coney Island, New York

MAIN ALLIES Suicide Squad, Poison Ivy

MAIN FOES The Joker

Harley's skin is bleached white, after The Joker pushed her into a vat of chemicals

Costume retains elements of a traditional harlequin design

HARLEY THE LEADER

After the disappearance of Rick Flag, Amanda Waller must select a new leader for the Suicide Squad. Katana seems like the obvious choice to lead, but Waller names Harley Quinn the leader of Task Force X. Harley is as surprised as anyone, but Deadshot agrees with Waller. Harley is the one who can unite them all and lead them into the most brutal missions.

HAWK AND DOVE
WAR AND PEACE

The Super-Heroic duo of Hawk and Dove are opposites: Hawk is warlike and aggressive, while Dove prefers to use nonviolence and reason to face problems. They must battle their enemies together if they are to defeat them. To access their powers, they need only to speak their own code names.

Mask features a hooked beak like a bird of prey

Cape resembles the wings of a dove

VITAL STATS

REAL NAME Henry Hall and Dawn Granger

OCCUPATION Super Heroes

HEIGHT 6 ft 1 in (1.85 m); 5 ft 9 in (1.75 m)

WEIGHT 197 lb (89 kg); 120 lb (54 kg)

BASE Washington, D.C.

MAIN ALLIES The Titans, Deadman

MAIN FOES Condor and Swan

PROTECTING THE PRESIDENT

Hawk and Dove are at an awards ceremony in the White House when villainous bird avatars Condor and Swan attack the President. Although the heroic duo save the President's life, Swan gets away. Condor's interrogation at the police station reveals that Hawk and Dove still have a lot to learn about their powers.

POWERS

The duo's powers are given to them by the Lords of Chaos and Order. Hawk has super-strength, speed, and durability, plus sharp claws, enhanced vision, and an accelerated healing factor. If Dove is not with him, Hawk can go into a rage. Dove has superhuman strength and intelligence and can fly. She can activate her powers only if she senses danger.

HAWKGIRL
HERO FOR THE AGES

After an encounter with powerful Nth Metal in the ancient Egyptian desert, Chay-ara and her partner Khufu gain incredible powers, including flight. Chay-ara is reborn many times over the millennia before becoming Kendra Saunders in the modern era. Kendra proves herself a worthy ally to the Justice League during one of Earth's darkest hours, and she joins them as Hawkgirl.

Following her encounter with the demon Barbatos, Hawkgirl's wings regrow as metal instead of feathers

VITAL STATS

REAL NAME Kendra Saunders

OCCUPATION Super Hero

HEIGHT 5 ft 6 in (1.68 m)

WEIGHT 131 lb (59 kg)

BASE Blackhawk Island

MAIN ALLIES Justice League, Hawkman, Council of Immortals

MAIN FOES Hath-Set, Barbatos

Helmet, gauntlets, and belt are made from Nth Metal

LADY BLACKHAWK

When Hawkgirl tries to prevent the Earth from sinking into the Dark Multiverse, she is transformed by the demon Barbatos into the evil Lady Blackhawk. However, Wonder Woman strikes her with the Lasso of Truth to make Hawkgirl remember her true identity. Back to her senses, Hawkgirl manages to summon her partner Hawkman and sets the heroes on the path to victory.

POWERS

Hawkgirl is immortal—when she dies, she is born again. In each life, she remembers the lives she led before, so she has built up a vast amount of knowledge. She has enhanced strength and durability and can use her razor-sharp wings to fly All her powers are derived from Nth Metal.

HAWKMAN
WINGED WONDER

Archaeologist Carter Hall is also the Super Hero Hawkman. His many powers come from the mystical Nth Metal. Carter discovers that he has been reincarnated many times throughout the course of human history, not only on Earth but also across the Multiverse on planets like Thanagar and Krypton.

Hawkman's weapon of choice is his powerful Nth Metal mace

Hawkman's wings are made from feathers laced with Nth Metal

POWERS

Nth Metal gives Hawkman amazing powers, like flight, super-strength, and enhanced vision, and also enables him to live for centuries in different lives. He accumulates great wisdom through the years, and always finds his true love, Hawkgirl, who is also immortal. He can heal rapidly from wounds.

JOURNEY TO THE DARK

Carter Hall wants to know more about the Nth Metal that changed him so much. Discovering a link to the Dark Multiverse, he manages to travel there, leaving details of his findings in a hidden journal. But Carter is trapped by the demon Barbatos and turned into a monster. Eventually Hawkgirl manages to reach him. On hearing her voice, Hawkman's true self returns, and he attacks Barbatos.

VITAL STATS

REAL NAME Carter Hall

OCCUPATION Super Hero, archaeologist

HEIGHT 6 ft 1 in (1.85 m)

WEIGHT 195 lb (88 kg)

BASE Blackhawk Island

MAIN ALLIES Hawkgirl, Justice League, Council of Immortals

MAIN FOES Hath-Set, Barbatos

HEAT WAVE
FIRE STARTER

Mick Rory is a pyromaniac (someone obsessed with fire), so it is not surprising that he chooses extreme heat as his weapon. He is an enemy of The Flash (Barry Allen) and a member of the Rogues criminal gang, carrying out heists around Central City as the villain known as Heat Wave.

Goggles protect Heat Wave's eyes from the effects of his weapons

VITAL STATS

REAL NAME Mick Rory
OCCUPATION Criminal
HEIGHT 5 ft 11 in (1.80 m)
WEIGHT 179 lb (81 kg)
BASE Central City
MAIN ALLIES The Rogues
MAIN FOES The Flash (Barry Allen)

Heat Wave's battle suit is heat-resistant

POWERS

Heat Wave's weapons produce such high temperatures that he can melt metal. His love of watching fires sometimes causes him to let his power get out of control. Heat Wave is an extremely dangerous crook, and other villains have tried to capture him to turn him into a human firebomb.

DEFEAT FROM VICTORY

After the Rogues pull off what they plan to be their final heist in Central City, Heat Wave can't resist paying one last visit to his burned-out family home. The Flash (Barry Allen) confronts him, but Heat Wave blasts him and escapes. Barry isn't hurt and follows Heat Wave, who leads him to the other Rogues.

HIPPOLYTA
AMAZON QUEEN

Hippolyta is the ruler of the warrior race of Amazons on the island of Themyscira. She is also the mother of Wonder Woman, a child fathered by the god Zeus. When Steve Trevor accidentally discovers the island, Hippolyta realizes with pride and sadness that she must send her daughter to "Man's World."

Crown denotes her rank as queen

VITAL STATS

REAL NAME Hippolyta

OCCUPATION Queen of the Amazons

HEIGHT 5 ft 10 in (1.78 m)

WEIGHT 150 lb (68 kg)

BASE Themyscira

MAIN ALLIES The Amazons, Goddesses of Olympus

MAIN FOES Circe, Heroules

Staff also functions as a handy weapon

LEADING FROM THE FRONT

When trouble comes to Themyscira, Queen Hippolyta is not the kind of monarch to let others do the fighting for her. She is a proud warrior, always on the front lines leading her people by example. Hippolyta even defeats Darkseid's daughter, Grail, when the villain attempts to lead an invasion of Themyscira.

Girdle is a magical belt that was a gift from the gods

KRAK

POWERS

With millennia of experience, Hippolyta is a weapons expert and skilled hand-to-hand fighter. Her weapon of choice is a broadsword. She has enhanced strength, intellect, and accelerated healing. Hippolyta is also immortal.

HUNTRESS
DAUGHTER OF THE MOB

Helena Bertinelli is a former secret agent who becomes the Super Hero and vigilante Huntress. Her first mission is to settle a very personal grudge with a mafia family—former friends turned deadly rivals of her own family. Huntress is at first willing to use lethal force, but after joining the Birds of Prey team, she softens her approach.

Masked Huntress is very protective of her secret identity, at first not even revealing it to her Birds of Prey allies

POWERS

Although she has no superpowers, Huntress is a former agent of the Spyral organization and is trained in the various arts of espionage. Helena is skilled in the use of many weapons, particularly the crossbow, and is also an expert motorcyclist and helicopter pilot.

Huntress wears a unique overcoat, with a hood to better hide her face

NEW FAMILY

Huntress is seeking revenge for her family when she runs into Batgirl and Black Canary, the Birds of Prey. At first Huntress is not keen on the idea of a team-up, but when Batgirl and Black Canary save her from the evil Snake Men, she realizes that they fight better together. Huntress joins the Birds of Prey, and her new teammates are among the very few people she trusts.

VITAL STATS

REAL NAME Helena Bertinelli

OCCUPATION Vigilante

HEIGHT 5 ft 11 in (1.98 m)

WEIGHT 130 lb (59 kg)

BASE Gotham City

MAIN ALLIES Birds of Prey, Nightwing

MAIN FOES Santo Cassamento, Mister Minos, Oracle

THE IMMORTAL MEN
HUMANITY'S SECRET PROTECTORS

Since the dawn of humanity, a secret war has been going on between the heroic Immortal Men and the evil House of Conquest. The Immortal Man has spent millennia cherry-picking metahumans for his team and giving them just enough of his power to make them live forever. However, following a disastrous clash with the enemy, their numbers are reduced to just four of the Immortal Man's chosen.

LAST HOPE

The Immortal Men need to find and protect a young man named Caden Park, who is just starting to realize that he might have metahuman powers. However, the House of Conquest also seeks Caden and has found a terrifying new ally in the Batman Who Laughs.

MEMBERS INCLUDE

1. GHOST FIST Cyril wields ghost energy and used to oppose organized crime in 1920s New York City.

2. TIMBER Born in the 19th century, Keshena is a hero of the Menominee Nation and can change her size.

3. STRAY This hero is a victim of experiments that turned her into a monster in the 1990s.

4. RELOAD Patrick has the power to alter time and is an excellent marksman.

IRIS WEST
ACE REPORTER

Top investigative journalist Iris West is an integral part of the Flash Family. She is the girlfriend of the first Flash (Barry Allen) and aunt to the other Flash (Wally West) and Kid Flash (Wallace R. West). When any family member is threatened, Iris defends them fiercely.

Iris West has red hair like her nephew, Wally

COLD RECEPTION

While in the 21st century, Iris is accused of killing Reverse-Flash in the 25th century. Her arresting officers are a future version of the villainous Rogues gang called the Renegades. At first, Iris is furious as "Commander Cold" takes aim with his cold gun at both Flashes. Later, Iris agrees to go into the future and face tr[ ] return, Cold promises to use future technology to help Wally West, who is suffering from "time seizures."

POWERS

Iris has no superpowers but is an extremely talented newspaper reporter with a knack for getting to the bottom of a story. Her investigative skills rival any found in the Central City Police Department. After spending time traveling around Markovia by motorcycle, Iris is also a capable mechanic.

VITAL STATS

REAL NAME Iris Ann West

OCCUPATION Investigative journalist

HEIGHT 5 ft 6 in (1.68 m)

WEIGHT 130 lb (59 kg)

BASE Central City

MAIN ALLIES The Flash Family

MAIN FOES Reverse-Flash, Zoom

JIMMY OLSEN
SUPERMAN'S PAL

Jimmy Olsen is a reporter and photographer, and an integral part of the team at *The Daily Planet* in Metropolis. Olsen is a good journalist, but he sometimes draws the wrath of editor Perry White. When Clark Kent starts working at the *Planet*, he and Jimmy hit it off and end up becoming good friends. Olsen is even best man at Clark's wedding to Lois Lane.

VITAL STATS

REAL NAME James "Jimmy" Olsen

OCCUPATION Photojournalist

HEIGHT 6 ft 2 in (1.88 m)

WEIGHT 210 lb (95 kg)

BASE Metropolis

MAIN ALLIES Superman, Lois Lane, Perry White

MAIN FOES Braniac, Ultraman

CLOSE CONFIDANT

During a lunch together, Jimmy confides in Clark that he has given away to the needy the fortune he inherited from his parents. Clark praises Jimmy's selflessness and reveals that he also has a secret ... that he is Superman! Jimmy is amazed and delighted that his friend is also his biggest hero.

POWERS

Jimmy Olsen does not have superpowers, although sometimes being near Superman can lead him into temporarily acquiring unusual abilities. He is a good reporter and excellent photographer. Olsen has a generous spirit and is determined to make it in life on his own talents.

Olsen is rarely seen without his camera around his neck, ready for when the next scoop comes along

Jimmy Olsen's signal watch sends out a hypersonic noise that only Superman can hear

JOHN CONSTANTINE
THE HELLBLAZER

Having studied magic and the occult since childhood, John Constantine becomes an accomplished mage. He wants to use his abilities to do the right thing, although sometimes his methods are rather questionable. Constantine is one of the founding members of supernatural super-team Justice League Dark.

VITAL STATS

REAL NAME John Constantine

OCCUPATION Magician, investigator

HEIGHT 6 ft (1.83 m)

WEIGHT 158 lb (72 kg)

BASE House of Mystery

MAIN ALLIES Justice League Dark, Swamp Thing

MAIN FOES Nick Necro, Cult of the Cold Flame, Blight

POWERS

Constantine is a powerful sorcerer whose talents go far beyond simple illusions. He can also summon and banish demons and control various forms of energy, including creating and firing electrical blasts. He is capable of mind control, teleportation, astral projection, and a host of other magical abilities.

Constantine's trademark trench coat is given to him by his mentor Nick Necro

LONDON CALLING

When a demon puts a curse on Constantine that will kill him if he stays in London, the mage heads to New York City. But Constantine returns when he craves a good curry and transfers the demon's curse to all 8 million Londoners. He trusts that his irritated—and psychic—former friend Mercury will save the day, which she does by speaking the demon's true name, Nybbas.

THE JOKER
CLOWN PRINCE OF CRIME

The Joker is Batman's nemesis, and their endless duel motivates The Joker far more than anything else. The Clown Prince of Crime sees himself as necessary for Batman to exist—after all, what would Batman do if he didn't have The Joker's crimes to stop? As well as being one of Batman's oldest enemies, The Joker is also the most mysterious, as nobody—even he himself—knows his true identity.

The Joker's skin is bleached white and his hair turned green after a fall into a vat of chemicals

No matter what terrible crime he is committing, The Joker's face is permanently smiling

VITAL STATS

REAL NAME Unknown
OCCUPATION Criminal
HEIGHT 6 ft (1.83 m)
WEIGHT 160 lb (73 kg)
BASE Gotham City
MAIN ALLIES Legion of Doom
MAIN FOES Batman, Batgirl, Red Hood

BEST MAN

An invitation to Batman and Catwoman's wedding is the hottest ticket in town for the metahuman community. The Joker is peeved that he has not received one, so he lures Batman to a church and pops the question—is he going to be the Dark Knight's best man? Before Batman can answer, a bomb planted by The Joker goes off. Luckily for Batman, Catwoman is on the scene to help.

POWERS

The Joker has an extremely rare metal named dionesium present in his body, appearing only at times of extreme injury. It enables him to heal from apparently lethal wounds. He likes to use weapons with a joke-shop flavor to them, like joy buzzers delivering painful bursts of electricity or a lapel flower shooting acid. He has also created Joker Venom, which leaves its victims wearing The Joker's big smile.

JONAH HEX
BOUNTY HUNTER OF THE OLD WEST

Bounty hunter Jonah Hex operates along the wild frontier of the American Old West. Though ruthless and brutal, he abides by a personal code that protects the innocent. Hex bears terrible scars on his face, legacy of a punishment from Native American Apaches. He is a lone wolf by nature but has a sharp-shooting girlfriend named Tallulah Black.

Hex's scars came from a red-hot Native American tomahawk

POWERS

Jonah Hex does not have metahuman powers, but his incredible marksmanship and quick-drawing ability verges on the superhuman. He is also an expert tracker and an adaptable and speedy learner of new skills. Hex rapidly picks up how to operate 21st-century technology, such as motor vehicles.

Hex's weapons of choice are single-action Colt .45 revolvers

FACE OF THE FUTURE

When Jonah Hex is accidentally transported to the 21st century, he tries to adjust to life in the future. Unfortunately, he winds up in a motorcycle accident. Hex wakes up from a coma in the hospital and discovers that doctors, using modern medicine, have healed his scarring and removed the cataract that had blinded his right eye.

VITAL STATS

REAL NAME Jonah Hex
OCCUPATION Bounty hunter
HEIGHT 5 ft 11 in (1.80 m)
WEIGHT 189 lb (86 kg)
BASE The American Frontier
MAIN ALLIES Tallulah Black
MAIN FOES Quentin Turnbull, El Papagayo, Vandal Savage

JUSTICE LEAGUE
THE WORLD'S GREATEST SUPER HEROES

The Justice League is a team of Earth's greatest Super Heroes. Its mission is to protect Earth from the most dangerous threats, those that are too much for just one hero to face. Following one such event (the invasion of Earth by villains from the Dark Multiverse), the Justice League strengthens its roster to deal with the aftermath. The team also appoints a new chairman, Martian Manhunter.

PSYCHIC BOARDROOM

Although its official headquarters is the rebuilt Hall of Justice in Washington, D.C., the Justice League can hold a meeting instantly, no matter where its members are. New leader Martian Manhunter uses his telepathy to join his teammates in a linking of minds and can create a "psychic boardroom." Here they can meet with their minds while their physical bodies remain elsewhere.

MEMBERS INCLUDE

1. **HAWKGIRL** Kendra is enhanced by the rare Nth Metal.

2. **MARTIAN MANHUNTER** The new chairman of the League is an alien telepath and shape-shifter.

3. **GREEN LANTERN (JOHN STEWART)** This former marine leads the Green Lantern Corps.

4. **CYBORG** Victor is powered by Mother Box tech.

5. **WONDER WOMAN** Diana is a powerful Amazonian warrior.

6. **BATMAN** The Dark Knight is the world's greatest detective.

7. **SUPERMAN** This Kryptonian powerhouse is a veteran member of the League.

8. **AQUAMAN** This mighty hero is also King of Atlantis.

9. **THE FLASH (BARRY ALLEN)** Barry is the team's resident speedster.

JUSTICE LEAGUE OF AMERICA
A FRESH START

Following the Justice League's battle with the Suicide Squad, Batman realizes there is room for another team—one that shows the public that anyone can be a hero. He recruits a mixture of established heroes, reforming villains, young up-and-comers ... and Lobo. The team sets up home in the disused Justice League HQ in Happy Harbor. But there are a lot of big personalities on the roster, which inevitably leads to clashes.

EVOLUTION OF THE JUSTICE LEAGUE

The villain Chronos travels through time to prevent the God of Super Heroes from creating the idea of Super Heroes on Earth. The Justice League of America manages to save the day, and every Super Hero who has ever existed. The team decides to take the concept of Super Heroes to a new level, creating the Justice Foundation to work with ordinary people in a "superhuman think tank".

MEMBERS INCLUDE

1. **BATMAN** The Dark Knight brings the team together.

2. **THE RAY** This hero has incredible light-manipulation powers.

3. **BLACK CANARY** Dinah Drake-Lance has a powerful super-sonic scream.

4. **FROST** This reformed villain drops the "Killer" part of her name as she tries to do good.

5. **VIXEN** Thanks to a magical totem, Mari McCabe can take on any animal powers.

6. **LOBO** The invulnerable, super-strong bounty hunter is the muscle of the group.

7. **THE ATOM** Ryan Choi is the team's tech guru.

JUSTICE LEAGUE OF CHINA
PROTECTING THE EAST

The Justice League of China contains heroes with similar powers to the original Justice League. Its members meet their namesakes when they go to the US in search of an ancient artifact. Assembled by the secretive Ministry of Self-Reliance, the Justice League of China later breaks away from the government. The team becomes an independent group devoted to bringing balance and harmony to their nation.

MEMBERS OF THE JLC

1. DRAGONSON Ahn Kwang-Jo wields a North Korean relic that gives him superhuman aquatic powers.

2. SUPER-MAN Kenan has Superman's powers and leads the team.

3. WONDER-WOMAN This heroic snake has taken on human form.

4. ROBINBOT Bat-Man created this powerful robot sidekick.

5. FLASH Avery Ho gets her powers from a Speed Force Storm.

6. BAT-MAN Wang Baixi invents many gadgets to help the team.

LETTING GO

When Super-Man accidentally traps himself and the rest of the team in the Realm of Ghosts, they must all face manifestations of their worst fears for the future. Super-Man realizes that he needs to let go of personal sadness from his past and appreciate the happiness that he could have now. His epiphany enables the team to return to the real world.

JUSTICE SOCIETY OF AMERICA
GOLDEN AGE HEROES

The Justice Society of America, or JSA, is the world's first super-team. Heroes of a Golden Age, its members inspire those that come after them. The founding teammates are recruited by the US President to fight a hidden battle during World War II. As the years pass, the team grows and changes. The older members train the next generation of heroes, instilling in them the same high moral standards they have always had.

JSA VS. JSA

When the powerful being Gog tries to make Earth a better place, the Justice Society is divided. Some members, led by Green Lantern Alan Scott, are concerned that Gog is breaking their no-kill code to get rid of evil people. But more warlike members, like Hawkman, agree with Gog's methods. The two factions are headed for a showdown.

MEMBERS INCLUDE

ALAN SCOTT, THE ATOM, ATOM SMASHER, DOCTOR FATE, DOCTOR MID-NITE, HAWKMAN, HOURMAN, JAY GARRICK, JESSE QUICK, JOHNNY THUNDER, LIGHTNING, MISTER TERRIFIC, POWER GIRL, SANDMAN, STARGIRL, WILDCAT

KATANA
SAMURAI WARRIOR

Tatsu Yamashiro becomes an agent of vengeance after the tragic loss of her family. Armed with a mystical weapon called Soultaker, she embarks on a quest for justice as Katana, guided by the souls trapped in her blade. Eventually she becomes one of the only willing recruits to the Suicide Squad and its field commander.

Mask is decorated with the rising sun symbol of Katana's native Japan

Souls trapped within her sword whisper to Katana

VITAL STATS

REAL NAME Tatsu Yamashiro

OCCUPATION Government black ops agent

HEIGHT 5 ft 2 in (1.57 m)

WEIGHT 96 lb (44 kg)

BASE Belle Reve Penitentiary

MAIN ALLIES Suicide Squad, Batman, The Outsiders

MAIN FOES Takeo Yamashiro, Lady Eve

FASTER THAN A SPEEDING BULLET

When the Black Vault causes the sane occupants of Belle Reve Penitentiary to lose their minds, Suicide Squad commander Rick Flag shoots Amanda Waller. He thinks he has killed her but is amazed to find that Katana managed to get in front of her and stop the bullet with her sword.

POWERS

Katana is one of the finest sword combatants in the world. She has also been training in martial arts since childhood. Her sword, Soultaker, is haunted by the souls of those it has slain. The weapon chooses Katana to be its bearer and to seek justice for those imprisoned within it.

Wallace West is a big fan of The Flash (Barry Allen). When Wallace gets a connection to the Speed Force, he goes to his hero for help. Barry senses Wallace's potential and takes him under his wing, mentoring him as the new Kid Flash.

SAVING WALLY

Wallace West meets Wally West, his predecessor as Kid Flash. The two share a bond through the Speed Force, and later Wallace senses that Wally is in trouble. Kid Flash rushes to Wally's side and discovers that his heart has stopped. Wallace performs a special kind of CPR, healing Wally with the power of the Speed Force.

POWERS

Wallace can tap into the Speed Force energy to move at super-speed and give himself superhuman agility, reflexes, and stamina. He has learned to channel the Speed Force to fire energy blasts. Kid Flash can take away speed from other moving objects, like bullets, slowing them down or stopping them completely.

Kid Flash uses the Speed Force to generate his suit

VITAL STATS

REAL NAME Wallace Rudolph West

OCCUPATION Super Hero

HEIGHT 5 ft 7 in (1.70 m)

WEIGHT 130 lb (59 kg)

BASE Central City

MAIN ALLIES The Flash Family, Teen Titans

MAIN FOES Godspeed

The Speed Force energy channeled by Kid Flash shows up as red lightning

KILLER CROC
KING OF THE SEWERS

Waylon Jones suffers from a genetic condition that gives him a reptilian appearance and superhuman abilities. Going by the name of Killer Croc, he lives in the sewer systems under Gotham City, angry and bitter over his rejection by society. Croc is later recruited to the Suicide Squad, where he finds acceptance of a sort from his new teammates.

VITAL STATS

REAL NAME Waylon Jones

OCCUPATION Super-villain, former carnival wrestler

HEIGHT 6 ft 5 in (1.96 m)

WEIGHT 385 lb (175 kg)

BASE Gotham City

MAIN ALLIES Suicide Squad, Catwoman

MAIN FOES Batman, Bane

Extremely sharp teeth are formidable weapons

A SOFTER SIDE

Despite his terrifying appearance, Killer Croc is not just a straight-up super-villain. He protects the poor and homeless of Gotham City, creating a refuge for them in his subterranean kingdom. Killer Croc also starts a loving relationship with Suicide Squad teammate June Moone.

POWERS

Killer Croc's genetic condition gives him incredible strength and also superhuman speed, especially while swimming. His sharp claws and fangs are formidable weapons in a fight. Croc's prowess in hand-to-hand combat also proved very useful in his former career, wrestling in a carnival sideshow.

Killer Croc is the Suicide Squad's strongest member

KILLER FROST
ICE QUEEN

Scientist Dr. Caitlin Snow is transformed into Killer Frost in a lab accident. At first, she is a villain, draining the body heat from people to keep herself alive. She is arrested and sent to Belle Reve Penitentiary, where she is coerced into joining the Suicide Squad. However, she retains enough of her old self to reject evil. She starts using the code name Frost and tries to be a hero.

The change in Caitlin's genetic makeup causes her skin and hair to turn to an icy shade of blue-white

TRUE HERO

When Max Lord tries to uncover a dark secret hidden in Killer Frost's soul, he finds instead her desire to reform her ways. Frost uses his momentary distraction to strike back at him, channeling the energies of the Justice League and Suicide Squad to blast the villain. Afterward, Batman releases her from the Suicide Squad and makes her the first member of his new Justice League of America.

Caitlin emits frosty projectiles from her hands

POWERS

Caitlin can fire icy shards from her hands, freeze others with her touch, and create ice storms. She also has a genius-level intellect and was one of the brightest scientists working at S.T.A.R. Labs until her transformation into Killer Frost.

VITAL STATS

REAL NAME Caitlin Snow

OCCUPATION Scientist, Super Hero, former criminal

HEIGHT 5 ft 4 in (1.63 m)

WEIGHT 123 lb (56 kg)

BASES Sanctuary; Happy Harbor, Rhode Island

MAIN ALLIES Justice League of America, Suicide Squad

MAIN FOES The Extremists, Queen of Fables, Chronos

KILOWOG
GREEN LANTERN DRILL INSTRUCTOR

Kilowog is a bulky, powerful Green Lantern and the only survivor of the planet Bolovax Vik. Devastated by the loss of his homeworld, Kilowog takes comfort in the comradeship of the Green Lantern Corps. For much of his time as a Lantern, he is responsible for training new recruits, or "poozers" as Kilowog likes to call them.

Green power ring is powered by the force of Kilowog's will

FOR THE CORPS

When the Guardians of the Universe decide to purge the Green Lantern Corps of free will, Kilowog manages to escape them. He assembles his own team on the Corps homeworld of Oa to fight back against their former masters. While Guy Gardner distracts the Guardians, Kilowog frees his trapped comrades and sends word of the plot to other Lanterns.

Kilowog's size, strength, and formidable appearance come from his Bolovaxian heritage

POWERS

Kilowog uses his Green Lantern power ring to enable him to fly and create hard light constructs. As a Bolovaxian, Kilowog has superhuman strength and durability even without his ring. He would also be able to communicate mentally with other Bolovaxians, if any had survived.

VITAL STATS

REAL NAME Kilowog

OCCUPATION Green Lantern trainer

HEIGHT 8 ft 3 in (2.51 m)

WEIGHT 720 lb (327 kg)

BASE Mogo

MAIN ALLIES Green Lantern Corps

MAIN FOES Sinestro Corps

KING SHARK
DANGER IN THE WATER

Nanaue, a.k.a. King Shark, is the son of Kamo, an individual who thinks he is an ancient Hawaiian deity. King Shark is taken by Amanda Waller and raised to adulthood in Belle Reve Penitentiary. When he is fully grown, he joins the Suicide Squad. He later breaks free of Waller's control and starts a new life underwater.

King Shark also has sharp claws

POWERS

King Shark can live underwater indefinitely and can also swim extremely fast. Unlike true sharks, he can also survive on land. He has superhuman strength, stamina, and durability, as well as razor-sharp teeth.

Head mimics the hammerhead shark species in appearance

VITAL STATS

REAL NAME Nanaue

OCCUPATION Criminal

HEIGHT 7 ft 2 in (2.18 m)

WEIGHT 380 lb (172 kg)

BASE Atlantis

MAIN ALLIES N.E.M.O., Black Manta, Suicide Squad

MAIN FOES Aquaman, Teen Titans

UNLIKELY ALLIES

As Corum Rath usurps the throne of Atlantis, King Shark is busy trying to rule the city's criminal underworld. King Shark joins Aquaman as an unlikely hero in the rebellion against Rath. King Shark even helps to destroy the magical barrier called the Crown of Thorns that prevents anyone from entering, or leaving, Atlantis.

KRYPTO
SUPER-DOG

Krypto is the last pet of Krypton. This caninelike animal is used as a test subject for a rocket Jor-El creates to save his son Kal-El from Krypton's destruction. The pet's rocket is knocked off course, but eventually he arrives on Earth to be reunited with Kal-El and becomes the Kent family's beloved pet. Unlike a regular dog, Krypto also has amazing Kryptonian superpowers.

POWERS

Krypto's physiology is affected by Earth's sun in the same way as Superman's, so he has incredible powers on the planet. He has heat vision, freeze breath, and the power of flight. Krypto also has heightened senses, super-strength, durability, and stamina. Like Superman, Krypto is vulnerable to Kryptonite and magic.

While Krypto looks like a dog, he is actually a Kryptonian creature

Krypto wears Superman's S-shield on his collar

VITAL STATS

REAL NAME Krypto

OCCUPATION Pet

HEIGHT 2 ft 2 in (0.66 m)

WEIGHT 40 lb (18 kg)

BASE Metropolis

MAIN ALLIES Superman, Superboy, Lois Lane

MAIN FOES The Eradicator

DOG VS. ERADICATOR

When the Kryptonian robot Eradicator tries to destroy the human half of Superman's son, Jonathan, Krypto leaps into action to save his master. The loyal pet puts his body in front of the Eradicator's ray and is sucked into another dimension. Superman frees Krypto, and the two take down the Eradicator together.

LADY SHIVA
DEADLY ASSASSIN

Sandra Wu-San is also known as Lady Shiva and is a deadly assassin. She is one of the world's most skilled hand-to-hand fighters and is even capable of defeating Batman. Lady Shiva also leads the secretive League of Shadows organization.

VITAL STATS

REAL NAME Sandra Wu-San

OCCUPATION Assassin

HEIGHT 5 ft 8 in (1.73 m)

WEIGHT 115 lb (52 kg)

BASE Mobile

MAIN ALLIES League of Shadows, League of Assassins

MAIN FOES Batman, Robin, Nightwing

Dark clothing enables Shiva to hide in the shadows

A MOTHER'S DISAPPOINTMENT

Having watched her daughter from the shadows, Lady Shiva is impressed when Cassandra sneaks up on her. However, when mother and daughter engage in battle, Shiva is disappointed to see that Cassandra holds back. Lady Shiva sees this reluctance as a sign of weakness and a waste of her daughter's talents.

POWERS

Although Lady Shiva is deadly with her bare hands, she also uses various weapons, like throwing stars and katanas. Lady Shiva is a master in every known martial art, and even a few that have been lost to history. She is an expert at reading her opponents' body language to work out their weak spots.

LANA LANG
SUPERWOMAN

Lana Lang comes from Smallville and is a childhood friend of Clark Kent. She knows about his powers and helps him learn to use them. As an adult, Lana goes into engineering before embarking on a career in the media. She later acquires metahuman powers and becomes a hero code named Superwoman.

Lana has an S-shield on her suit that represents the House of El

VITAL STATS

REAL NAME Lana Lang

OCCUPATION Journalist, Super Hero

HEIGHT 5 ft 7 in (1.70 m)

WEIGHT 127 lb (58 kg)

BASE Metropolis

MAIN ALLIES The Superman Family

MAIN FOES Lena Luthor

DIFFERENT KIND OF HERO

After Lana becomes Superwoman, she discovers that her powers are making her sick. Superwoman hesitates when a previously hostile A.I. named Midnight offers her the chance at a fresh start without powers. But Lana realizes that she can still be a hero without powers and allows Midnight to take them in order to save her life.

POWERS

As Superwoman, Lana can convert solar energy into electromagnetic power and fire electrical blasts at her enemies. She is super-strong, durable, and can even fly. Lana is also a gifted electrical engineer and journalist.

LEAGUE OF SHADOWS
SHIVA'S ASSASSINS

The League of Shadows is an even more secretive offshoot of the League of Assassins. Formerly led by Rā's al Ghūl, the League of Shadows is now under the command of the deadly Lady Shiva. Its members seek destruction through chaos but never take credit for their actions. The League of Shadows remains behind the scenes, an organization so mysterious that at first even Batman believes it to be no more than a myth.

MEMORY LOSS

Rā's al Ghūl breaks into the Batcave to reveal the truth about the League of Shadows to Batman—not only is the group real, but Batman has found out about it on three separate occasions. Each time, Rā's used magic to wipe Batman's memory of the League, leading the hero to wonder what else Rā's might have erased.

MEMBERS INCLUDE

LADY SHIVA, RĀ'S AL GHŪL, MANY NAMELESS ASSASSINS

LEGION OF SUPER-HEROES
HEROES OF THE FUTURE

The Legion of Super-Heroes comes from 1,000 years in the future. Its members are a group of youngsters from across the universe, chosen to join an exclusive team because of their special powers. At first, the Legion's main purpose is to protect wealthy businessman R. J. Brande. However, the team's talents are soon noticed by the authorities, and its members are deputized into the Science Police to protect the United Planets.

HERO OF HEROES
The Legion's members are huge fans of a Super Hero of the past—Superman. Saturn Girl, Lightning Lad, and Cosmic Boy use a Time Bubble devised by Brainiac 5 to travel back to 21st-century Metropolis. They want to meet the Man of Steel and hopefully recruit him to their team. But a mysterious dark force pushes them back into the future before they can make contact.

MEMBERS INCLUDE

1. LIGHTNING LAD
2. COSMIC BOY
3. ULTRA BOY
4. SATURN GIRL
5. INVISIBLE KID
6. TRIPLICATE GIRL
7. COLOSSAL BOY
8. BRAINIAC 5
9. PHANTOM GIRL
10. CHAMELEON BOY

LENA LUTHOR
HER BROTHER'S PRISONER

Lena Luthor is a genius scientist with a ruthless streak. Her brother Lex is ashamed of his failure to find a cure for her paralysis, so he hides her away in his lab at LexCorp. Lena is furious and resentful at her imprisonment. When she manages to escape, she wants revenge on Lex.

POWERS

Lena Luthor has an intellect far in excess of her brother's. She succeeds where he fails by creating an army of Bizarresses using her own DNA and that of the evil Superwoman from Earth-3. In her warsuit, she has super-strength and durability, among many other abilities.

Lena uses a wheelchair following her paralysis

Lena often dresses smartly

ULTRAWOMAN

Lex Luthor's attempt to cure Lena's paralysis using energy from Superman fails but leaves her with an even more advanced intellect than before. Lena cures herself then utilizes a giant battlesuit to turn herself into Ultrawoman. Her goal is to erase her brother Lex's achievements from history and claim them all as her own, "stolen" from her when he hid her away.

VITAL STATS

REAL NAME Lena Luthor
OCCUPATION Super-villain
HEIGHT 5 ft 8 in (1.73 m)
WEIGHT 130 lb (59 kg)
BASE Metropolis
MAIN ALLIES Bizarress Army
MAIN FOES Lex Luthor, Superwoman

LEX LUTHOR
SUPERMAN'S ARCHENEMY

Lex Luthor is a billionaire businessman who lives in Metropolis. When Superman first becomes a Super Hero, Luthor is deeply suspicious of this alien with incredible powers and resolves to defeat him. Luthor's main concern is that the Man of Steel might get in the way of his own ambitions, but Luthor will also defend humanity when called upon.

Lex's baldness is a mystery—it may have been caused by a lab accident or could just be hereditary

SUPER LEX

With Superman gone, Lex cannot resist stepping into his shoes and done a warsuit bearing the hero's S-shield. He even buys *The Daily Planet* so he can get his hands on Superman's cape, which is on show in the lobby. Lex claims he wants to make his sister proud, but it is possible that a desire for personal glory may also play a part ...

Lex often dresses like the successful businessman that he is

POWERS

Lex Luthor is one of the most intelligent people on Earth. He has used his engineering genius to create a series of warsuits, which are designed to enable him to take on the otherwise far more powerful Superman. His warsuits usually contain some kind of Kryptonite weapon.

VITAL STATS

REAL NAME Lex Luthor

OCCUPATION Businessman, megalomaniac

HEIGHT 6 ft 2 in (1.88 m)

WEIGHT 210 lb (95 kg)

BASE Metropolis

MAIN ALLIES Legion of Doom, Mercy Graves

MAIN FOES Superman, the Superman Family, Justice League

LIVEWIRE
PURE ENERGY

While trying to take control of Metropolis's power system, vlogger Leslie Willis is accidentally transformed into Livewire, a being of pure electricity. She embarks on a new career as a super-villain. Even Superman has trouble stopping her before Batman lends a hand by devising an energy trap. Livewire is then imprisoned in Stryker's Island Penitentiary.

Livewire's hands glow with electricity as she is preparing to fire an energy bolt

When she has used up all her electrical energy, Livewire's body appears human again

VITAL STATS

REAL NAME Leslie Willis

OCCUPATION Super-villain, former vlogger

HEIGHT 5 ft 6 in (1.68 m)

WEIGHT 130 lb (59 kg)

BASE Metropolis

MAIN ALLIES Secret Society of Super-Villains

MAIN FOES Superman, Batman, Batgirl

BATMAN FRIED

Livewire escapes Stryker's Island and finds herself in Gotham City, where she heads for the power plant. She is cornered by Commissioner Jim Gordon who is in a Batman mech suit. Unluckily for Jim, his Batsuit is all too vulnerable to electrical attack, and Livewire gets the upper hand. However, while Livewire takes a break to recharge, Batgirl arrives and stops her.

POWERS

Livewire absorbs electricity and uses it to power herself. She can fire bolts of lightning, powerful enough to get the better of Superman. She is also very strong against anyone with tech-based powers, as her electricity fries their circuits. Livewire can travel through wires in her electrical form.

LOBO
THE MAIN MAN

Lobo is thought to be the last survivor of the planet Czarnia. He makes his living as a bounty hunter, never giving up until he has completed his mission and earned his paycheck. Batman disagrees with Lobo's methods but recognizes Lobo's strength and recruits him for his new Justice League of America team.

Fully grown Czarnians have red eyes with no pupils

Lobo uses a range of weapons, but his favorite is a hook on a long chain

VITAL STATS

REAL NAME (Unpronounceable)

OCCUPATION Bounty hunter

HEIGHT 6 ft 6 in (1.98 m)

WEIGHT 305 lb (138 kg)

BASE Mobile

MAIN ALLIES Justice League of America, Batman

MAIN FOES Maxwell Lord, Amanda Waller, Gusano Tribb

SAVE THE DOLPHINS

The only creatures that Lobo seems to feel genuine affection for are space dolphins, and he protects them with a fierce devotion. When their homeworld is threatened by a rogue Czarnian, Lobo travels there through space with Black Canary to save them. Using Canary's cry as a distraction, Lobo gathers a team of dolphins to help him defeat the villain.

POWERS

Lobo is incredibly strong and has an advanced healing factor that enables him to survive virtually any injury. He even recovers after a Suicide-Squad-style brain-bomb is exploded in his head. He is immortal, simply for the reason that he is not allowed into either heaven or hell.

LOIS LANE
PRIZE-WINNING JOURNALIST

Lois Lane is the best reporter at Metropolis newspaper *The Daily Planet*. She is passionate about her job and often gives her long-suffering editor, Perry White, a hard time when he disagrees with a story she is working on. Lois is married to fellow journalist Clark Kent, who also happens to be Superman. They have a son together named Jonathan.

Lois usually dresses in smart clothes for her career but has been known to don a Super Hero suit

POWERS

Lois does not have superpowers, but she is an exceptional investigative journalist. She is dedicated to the truth and relentless when it comes to running down a story. Lois is also fiercely loyal and protective of her family. Raised by an army officer, she was taught basic combat skills as a child.

BAT-LOIS

Superman takes Lois and their son, Jon, to a secret Batcave on the moon, hoping to hide them from the villainous Eradicator. But the evil Kryptonian robot finds them and transports Superman to another dimension. Jon is cornered by the Eradicator, so Lois dons a Hellbat mech suit and battles the foe with a mother's protective fury.

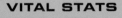

VITAL STATS

REAL NAME Lois Lane

OCCUPATION Journalist

HEIGHT 5 ft 7 in (1.70 m)

WEIGHT 120 lb (54 kg)

BASE Metropolis

MAIN ALLIES Superman, Superboy, Perry White

MAIN FOES Lex Luthor, Mister Mxyzptlk, Intergang

MAD HATTER
MIND-CONTROLLING MADMAN

Jervis Tetch is obsessed with the story of *Alice's Adventures in Wonderland* by Lewis Carroll. Dressing himself as Mad Hatter, he also recruits henchmen with connections to the book—Tweedledum and Tweedledee and the White Rabbit. Mad Hatter uses his mind-controlling abilities to commit crazy crimes in Gotham City, which makes him an enemy of Batman.

Although Mad Hatter can use other methods to control people's minds, he favors a top hat with a special device in it

VITAL STATS

REAL NAME Jervis Tetch

OCCUPATION Criminal

HEIGHT 4 ft 8 in (1.42 m)

WEIGHT 149 lb (68 kg)

BASE Gotham City

MAIN ALLIES The Batman Who Laughs, Secret Society of Super-Villains

MAIN FOES Batman, Nightwing, Batgirl

MALICE IN WONDERLAND

Mad Hatter becomes obsessed with recreating a "perfect" day he had with a friend named Alice when they were at school. He builds his own version of Wonderland and uses mind control to force Gotham City's citizens to play the roles of characters from the famous story. But when Batman arrives, Mad Hatter's perfect day is ruined, and he ends up back behind bars.

POWERS

Mad Hatter is a master at controlling the human mind and has built devices to plant on others so that they will do his bidding. The power he can achieve using his genius is affected by his insanity, caused by dangerous chemicals he took to try to increase his height.

Mad Hatter bases his outfit on his fictional namesake

MAN-BAT
ACCIDENTAL VILLAIN

Dr. Kirk Langstrom is trying to use bat DNA to make a cure for deafness when he accidentally creates a serum that turns him—and anyone else who uses it—into a giant bat-creature. Although Langstrom is a good man, too much use of his Man-Bat serum makes his human side almost disappear. He is then a danger to friend and foe alike.

POWERS

As Man-Bat, Kirk Langstrom can fly and has superhuman strength, durability, and stamina. He also has the natural bat ability of echolocation, enabling him to fly rapidly through the dark city of Gotham City without crashing into anything. However, if he remains in Man-Bat form for too long, he loses control and becomes dangerous.

Man-Bat's claws are sharp weapons

Like a bat, Man-Bat has enlarged ears to enable him to use echolocation

VITAL STATS

REAL NAME Kirk Langstrom

OCCUPATION Scientist

HEIGHT 6 ft 1 in (1.85 m)

WEIGHT 201 lb (91 kg)

BASE Gotham City

MAIN ALLIES Francine Langstrom, Justice League Dark, Gotham Academy

MAIN FOES Batman, Emperor Penguin

THE CURE

When the Man-Bat serum gets into the wrong hands, it spreads like a virus through a Gotham City district, transforming hundreds of innocent people into Man-Bats. Kirk is remorseful for the carnage his creation has caused so comes up with a solution. He cancels out the virus with a new version that turns all the citizens back to normal but leaves himself stuck in his Man-Bat form.

MARTIAN MANHUNTER
SHAPE-SHIFTING ALIEN TELEPATH

Coming to Earth as one of the last surviving Martians, J'onn J'onzz becomes known as Martian Manhunter. His incredible powers make him a worthy addition to the Justice League, and he eventually becomes the team's chairman. His wisdom allows him to fully understand the threats posed to Earth and the wider Multiverse, and his kindness drives him to protect his teammates in any way he can.

Martian Manhunter is of the race of Martians with green skin rather than white

VITAL STATS

REAL NAME J'onn J'onzz

OCCUPATION Super Hero

HEIGHT 6 ft 7 in (2.01 m)

WEIGHT 300 lb (136 kg)

BASE Hall of Justice

MAIN ALLIES Justice League, Stargirl

MAIN FOES Ma'alefa'ak, Lex Luthor

DESTROYING THE MOON

Vandal Savage has concocted a plan to tear off the Earth's crust using the moon. As soon as Martian Manhunter discovers this, he knows that he must destroy the moon. Manhunter shape-shifts into a Quonar, an extinct moon-nester, and hurls himself at the moon, destroying it—but saving Earth.

POWERS

Martian Manhunter's powers are typical of a Martian. He has super-strength, speed, stamina, and durability. He can fly and fire energy blasts from his eyes. He is also a powerful telepath and shape-shifter. Manhunter's detective skills are almost on par with Batman's.

Martian Manhunter chooses a form that looks like an Earthling's idea of what a Martian should look like

MAXWELL LORD
BLACK KING

Max Lord is the leader—code named Black King—of the Checkmate organization. This shadowy group claims to be a global peace operation. Lord does not believe he should have to answer to anyone and that rules are just for other people. He would be dangerous enough without powers, but Lord also has metahuman abilities that help him control others.

Sometimes the strain of using his powers gives Max Lord a nosebleed

POWERS

Maxwell Lord has incredible telepathic powers. He can read people's minds and send them a mental "nudge" to try to make them act on their worst thoughts. Amanda Waller tricks Lord into getting sent to prison so that she can harness his abilities for her new Task Force XI.

Black tee is Lord's signature look

ECLIPSED

Max Lord steals a powerful diamond known as the Heart of Darkness, which is magically linked to the demon Eclipso. He uses the gem to take control of the Justice League and forces the team to conquer the US, achieving "peace." But the diamond's evil power is too much for Lord and he becomes possessed by Eclipso.

VITAL STATS

REAL NAME Maxwell Lord IV

OCCUPATION Head of Checkmate organization

HEIGHT 6 ft 2 in (1.88 m)

WEIGHT 185 lb (84 kg)

BASE Belle Reve Penitentiary

MAIN ALLIES Task Force XI

MAIN FOES Amanda Waller

MERA
ATLANTEAN QUEEN

Originally from the aquatic colony of Xebel, Mera is raised to be an assassin, her target: Aquaman. However, her mission is derailed when she falls in love with the hero, the two making the ultimate team. Mera's incredible water-manipulating abilities make her a powerful force for good. But her quick temper sometimes gets her in trouble with the surface-dwelling authorities.

Crown is a symbol of her royal status both in Xebel and Atlantis

POWERS

Mera can command water and form it into hard shapes, giving her the ability to fire lethal projectiles. She is super-strong and a phenomenally quick swimmer. In addition to her powers, Mera also received years of training in hand-to-hand combat during her childhood in Xebel.

ODD OOUPLE

Mera is chosen as Queen of Atlantis after Aquaman refuses to be monarch. While she is on the surface world, the throne is usurped by Corum Rath. Surprisingly, Mera teams up with her former enemy Ocean Master and travels to her home of Xebel to try to recruit an army. The duo must fight a sea monster to win the right to speak with the Xebel king.

Mera's signature look is a green, scaly suit

VITAL STATS

REAL NAME Mera

OCCUPATION Queen of Atlantis, Super Hero

HEIGHT 5 ft 9 in (1.75 m)

WEIGHT 160 lb (73 kg)

BASE Atlantis

MAIN ALLIES Aquaman, Justice League

MAIN FOES Dead King, Black Manta

METAL MEN
THE AI TEAM

The Metal Men are a team of unruly, but selfless and heroic, androids created by brilliant robotics scientist Dr. Will Magnus. The first artificial intelligences in the world, their personalities come from their "responsometers"—devices that were put into molten metal to create their physical forms. The Metal Men were originally intended for military use, but they refused to kill and escaped.

MEMBERS INCLUDE

1. LEAD While slow in movement and thought, Lead is very loyal.

2. PLATINUM This compassionate hero is very courageous.

3. IRON Strong Iron can't wait to fight.

4. GOLD This android is a little arrogant and the team's leader.

5. MERCURY This hero is rash and quick.

6. TIN Nervous Tin is really shy.

METAL HEROES

With the rest of the Justice League out of action, Cyborg calls on the Metal Men to help him battle Grid, an evil A.I. allied with the Crime Syndicate. When Grid gets hold of Mercury's responsometer, Grid is fascinated by it, wanting to know how it is that these robots can have emotions. As Cyborg goes toe to toe with Grid in the digital universe, the Metal Men defeat members of the Secret Society of Super-Villains.

METALLO
KRYPTONITE HEART

Soldier John Corben's body is destroyed during a battle with Superman, who is under the influence of an evil virus. However, Corben lives on as Metallo, a robot containing his downloaded consciousness. He blames Superman for what happened to him and seeks revenge. Metallo is powered by a heart made of Kryptonite, an apt symbol for the carnage he wants to bring to Superman.

Metallo is powered by his Kryptonite heart

POWERS

Metallo's cybernetic body gives him a range of superhuman abilities. He is super-strong and durable, and his Kryptonite heart enables him to fire dangerous blasts of the substance at Superman. Metallo has advanced senses and can scan the area around him for useful data.

Metallo's latest body is created for him by Cyborg Superman

HEART OF A HERO

Lois Lane manages to reprogram Metallo, so he only remembers his previous loyalty to her and her father—General Sam Lane. Metallo then serves as her personal bodyguard. When Superman is fighting Vandal Savage, and in a strange quirk of fate needs Kryptonite to boost his powers, Metallo offers his own Kryptonite heart. This noble sacrifice lets Superman win the day and defeat Savage.

VITAL STATS

REAL NAME John Corben

OCCUPATION Super-villain, soldier

HEIGHT 6 ft 5 in (1.96 m)

WEIGHT 200 lb (91 kg)

BASE Metropolis

MAIN ALLIES Cyborg Superman

MAIN FOES Superman, Supergirl

METAMORPHO
ELEMENT MAN

Archaeologist Rex Mason is sent by corrupt businessman Simon Stagg to retrieve the Orb of Ra. However, he is transformed by the combination of radiation from the Orb and a drug given to him by Stagg. Mason can now change his body into any element. He becomes a Super Hero, code named Metamorpho, and a member of teams like the Outsiders and the Terrifics.

VITAL STATS

REAL NAME Rex Mason

OCCUPATION Super Hero

HEIGHT 6 ft 6 in (1.98 m)

WEIGHT 200 lb (91 kg)

BASE Mobile

MAIN ALLIES The Terrifics, The Outsiders, Sapphire Stagg

MAIN FOES Simon Stagg, Java

Metamorpho dislikes his weird appearance despite the powers he has gained

Metamorpho's body usually appears as a combination of five elements

PERFECT PARTNER

Metamorpho is imprisoned in Simon Stagg's lab, but Stagg's daughter Sapphire helps him escape. Sapphire's biochemical knowledge is invaluable for Metamorpho, as he learns from her which elements are best to change into in different situations. The two become close and eventually start dating.

POWERS

Metamorpho can transform any part of his body into any element and also change his size and shape, just by focusing his mind. He can be in gas, liquid, or solid compositions. He is near-invulnerable, as his body adjusts to heal any wounds.

METRON
SEEKER OF KNOWLEDGE

Although Metron appears to be a New God allied to New Genesis, he is in fact neutral. During the war between the planets Apokolips and New Genesis, it is Metron who suggests exchanging Darkseid and Highfather's sons as guarantees for peace. Metron's sole desire is for knowledge, and he seeks it throughout the universe on his Mobius Chair.

OUT OF THE CHAIR

When the Justice League is fighting the Anti-Monitor, Metron arrives and carries the team to safety in the Mobius Chair. Wonder Woman uses her Lasso of Truth to discover that to defeat the Anti-Monitor, she must get Metron out of his chair. When she does, Batman sits in it to prevent it from vanishing and becomes the God of Knowledge.

VITAL STATS

REAL NAME Metron
OCCUPATION Explorer
HEIGHT 6 ft 1 in (1.85 m)
WEIGHT 190 lb (86 kg)
BASE New Genesis
MAIN ALLIES None
MAIN FOES None

Mysterious energy that powers the Mobius Chair gives off an eerie glow

POWERS

Metron has all the superhuman powers and immortality of any New God. His possession of the Mobius Chair means that he has access to vast knowledge. He also uses the chair to travel the universe, observing events large and small.

Mobius Chair is the source of Metron's knowledge and his means of transportation

MIRROR MASTER
MAN IN THE MIRROR

Sam Scudder is a key member of the Rogues and an enemy of The Flash (Barry Allen). When the team leader, Captain Cold, tries to upgrade his team's abilities, Sam gets trapped in the alternate dimension named Mirror World. Luckily, his fellow Rogue Golden Glider frees him.

POWERS

Mirror Master's powers come from his high-tech mirror gun. He is the Rogues' getaway expert, as his link to Mirror World gives the gang a speedy exit from any trouble. He can also create mirror constructs to fool enemies into thinking the Rogues are somewhere they are not. He can communicate with the other Rogues through any reflective surface.

VITAL STATS

REAL NAME Samuel "Sam" Joseph Scudder

OCCUPATION Criminal

HEIGHT 5 ft 10 in (1.78 m)

WEIGHT 175 lb (79 kg)

BASE Central City

MAIN ALLIES The Rogues

MAIN FOES The Flash (Barry Allen)

Mirror gun can turn opponents into shards of glass

ROGUES VS. MAN-BATS

The world is in chaos after the invasion of the Crime Syndicate, and so are the Rogues. Ending up in Gotham City, Mirror Master is searching a factory with teammate Heat Wave, hoping to find parts to build a new mirror gun. They are attacked by Man-Bats, but quick-thinking Mirror Master uses the many reflective surfaces in the building to send the creatures to Mirror World.

MISTER FREEZE
COOL CROOK

Victor Fries is a scientist trying to find a way of healing his beloved, Nora, who is very sick. He puts her into cryogenic stasis, but Fries' obsessive behavior leads to the funding for his research being stopped. When his lab is shut down, a terrible accident bathes Fries in cryogenic chemicals, leaving him only able to survive at low temperatures. Fries becomes the villainous Mister Freeze and still hopes to find a way of curing Nora.

Dome-shaped helmet protects Mister Freeze's head from high temperatures and attacks while still providing all-around visibility

Mister Freeze's eyes are protected by red goggles

VITAL STATS

REAL NAME Victor Fries

OCCUPATION Scientist, super-villain

HEIGHT 6 ft (1.83 m)

WEIGHT 190 lb (86 kg)

BASE Gotham City

MAIN ALLIES The Batman Who Laughs, Secret Society of Super-Villains

MAIN FOES Batman, Nightwing

POWERS

Mister Freeze uses his scientific knowledge to create an ice gun and a refrigeration suit, which gives him super-strength and durability. The suit also protects his cryogenics-infused body after the lab accident, keeping it stable at the very low temperatures it needs to survive.

WINTER HAS COME

Mister Freeze is released from Arkham Asylum by the villainous Batman Who Laughs and given an area of Gotham City to do with as he pleases. Freeze creates a frozen, "pure" landscape and guards it with Frost Giants. However, Freeze is defeated by a team consisting of Nightwing, Robin, Green Arrow, Harley Quinn, and Killer Croc.

MISTER MIRACLE
HOSTAGE OF DARKSEID

Scot is the son of Highfather, ruler of New Genesis. He goes to Apokolips as a hostage—part of a peace treaty between the warring worlds. Thrown into the slave pits by Darkseid, Scot finds happiness through a forbidden love with Big Barda. The two flee from Darkseid's wrath and end up on Earth, where Scot helps humankind as the hero Mister Miracle.

VITAL STATS

REAL NAME Scot Free
OCCUPATION Super Hero
HEIGHT 6 ft (1.83 m)
WEIGHT 185 lb (84 kg)
BASE Los Angeles, California
MAIN ALLIES Big Barda, Wonders of the World
MAIN FOES Darkseid

RETURN TO APOKOLIPS

Mister Miracle returns to Apokolips and uses his talent for lock-picking to break into Darkseid's throne room. He wants to find out what the evil tyrant is planning, but just as he finds the information he seeks, Darkseid arrives. They fight, and Darkseid gains the upper hand, but Mister Miracle manages to reach his Mother Box. He orders it to get him out of there, fast!

Mister Miracle's outfit uses colors that remind him of his homeworld, New Genesis

POWERS

Mister Miracle is an unrivaled escape artist, able to free himself from almost any prison or trap. His genius-level intellect also gives him a special knowledge of powerful Mother Box technology, and he even manages to build his own. Like all New Gods, Mister Miracle is immortal and possesses super-strength, durability, and agility.

Aero disks allow Mister Miracle to fly and can also be used as shields or throwing weapons

MISTER TERRIFIC
TERRIFIC BY NAME ...

Mister Terrific is not only one of the smartest guys on Earth, he is also an Olympic-level athlete and martial artist. He believes that the world is an unfair place and decides to use his brain and his fortune to make it fairer. After visiting the Dark Multiverse, Mister Terrific finds he has been forcibly bonded to fellow heroes Plastic Man, Metamorpho, and Phantom Girl.

TRUSTED FRIEND

When Batman begins investigating an ancient cosmic mystery, he doesn't even tell the rest of the Justice League, though he confides in Mister Terrific. Batman respects Mister Terrific's intellect so much that he asks him to gather data for him from Earth-2. When the two meet secretly in the Lunar Batcave, Mister Terrific manages to do the almost impossible and sneaks up on the Dark Knight!

VITAL STATS

REAL NAME Michael Holt

OCCUPATION Businessman, scientist, Super Hero

HEIGHT 6 ft 2 in (1.88 m)

WEIGHT 215 lb (98 kg)

BASE Los Angeles, California

MAIN ALLIES The Terrifics

MAIN FOES Simon Stagg

T-Spheres are often found floating near Mister Terrific, ready for use

Mister Terrific displays his motto, "Fair Play," on his jacket

POWERS

Mister Terrific's most powerful asset is his incredible intellect. He has mastered a wide range of academic subjects and uses his knowledge to create a variety of high-tech gadgets, most notably his multipurpose T-Spheres. These floating robots can be weapons, communication devices, or even allow Mister Terrific to fly.

MON-EL
LEGIONNAIRE OF VALOR

Mon-El is a member of the Legion of Super-Heroes and has acted as its field leader. As Mon-El is a native of Daxam, lead is toxic to him. He is rescued from the Phantom Zone by the Legion and cured of the lead poisoning he is suffering from. He then becomes a hero, using his powers to help others.

TEAM PLAYER

Thanks to a special serum, Mon-El can survive on planets where lead is found. Unfortunately, a rogue Daxamite—named the Renegade—gets hold of the serum and plans to use it to make Daxam the most powerful planet in the galaxy. Mon-El works with the rest of the Legionnaires to stop the Renegade in his tracks.

Gold disk cape fastenings are Mon-El's signature costume pieces

VITAL STATS

REAL NAME Lar Gand
OCCUPATION Legionnaire
HEIGHT 6 ft 2 in (1.88 m)
WEIGHT 200 lb (91 kg)
BASE Legion Headquarters
MAIN ALLIES Legion of Super-Heroes
MAIN FOES Time Trapper

POWERS

Mon-El is one of the most powerful members of the Legion of Super-Heroes. His powers as a Daxamite are very similar to Superman's. The yellow sun of Earth activates his super-strength, speed, and durability and enables him to fly. Mon-El also has heat and X-ray vision.

MONGUL
MIGHTY ALIEN TYRANT

Mongul believes that the strong have the right to rule the weak, and he seeks to make his own galactic empire. He is an alien from an unknown planet, which was ruined by a war that he started. Mongul then takes command of *Warworld*, a formidable battleship capable of destroying planets. Even after the loss of *Warworld*, Mongul is still a powerful foe.

MONGUL VS. THE JUSTICE LEAGUE

Mongul brings the Justice League to an arena, nullifies the team's powers, and forces them to fight giant robots. Batman figures out that each robot has a hidden failsafe in its mouth, which has been left by the slave who built it. By pushing these buttons and going inside the roboto, the heroes can pilot the machines. They can even combine them into a powerful battlebot, and Mongul flees the arena.

Mongul's armor has energy blast capabilities from its green segments

POWERS

Mongul is a super-strong alien who can fire beams of fire from his eyes. He can also project powerful energy blasts from his chest armor. Mongul is very intelligent and has created a parasitic plant to paralyze his enemies. He has even proven himself strong enough to take on the Justice League in battle.

VITAL STATS

REAL NAME Mongul

OCCUPATION Alien megalomaniac

HEIGHT 8 ft (2.44 m)

WEIGHT 1,125 lb (510 kg)

BASE The moon

MAIN ALLIES Cyborg Superman

MAIN FOES Superman, Green Lantern Corps, Justice League

MONITOR
PROTECTOR OF THE MULTIVERSE

Nix Uotan is the last of the Monitor race, super-beings of almost unimaginable power whose job it is to protect the Multiverse itself. He is aided in this task by a talking chimp named Mr. Stubbs. The two use a "shift-ship" named the *Ultima Thule* to travel between universes, investigating potential threats. The Monitor sometimes calls himself "Superjudge."

As Superjudge, the Monitor has glowing eyes with no pupils

POWERS

The Monitor's powers are almost too great for the human mind to understand. He can appear in any size he chooses and channel the power of many suns to create energy blasts. The Monitor can sense disturbances anywhere in the Multiverse and even alter reality itself.

SAVING THE MULTIVERSE

When the entire Multiverse is threatened by evil beings calling themselves the Gentry, the Monitor goes to confront them on Earth-7. When they demand that he hand himself over in exchange for the last hero on Earth-7— the Thunderer—the Monitor agrees. But the Thunderer returns with an army of heroes from across the Multiverse to release the Monitor and thank him for his sacrifice.

VITAL STATS

REAL NAME Nix Uotan

OCCUPATION Protector of the Multiverse

HEIGHT Variable

WEIGHT Variable

BASE House of Heroes

MAIN ALLIES Monitors, Harbinger, Mr. Stubbs

MAIN FOES Anti-Monitor, The Gentry

MR. MXYZPTLK
IMP FROM ANOTHER DIMENSION

The curiously named Mr. Mxyzptlk is an Imp from the Fifth Dimension, who can perform nearly any feat when he visits the Third Dimension. Here he meets Superman, who becomes Mxy's favorite target of pranks and tricks. He does not want to rule the universe or fight others but just to play games and have fun— although his idea of fun is often extremely troublesome!

Mr. Mxyzptlk has no fixed physical form but often chooses to appear as a small, comical-looking man

POWERS

Mr. Mxyzptlk is immensely powerful, although he mostly uses his abilities for tricks. He can warp reality itself and take on any physical form he chooses. However, his antics can be stopped by simple rules he sets himself, like someone saying his name backward—Kltpzyxm. Then he must return to the Fifth Dimension for 90 days.

Mr. Mxyzptlk can perform astounding feats of magic just by snapping his fingers

A NEW "CLARK KENT"

After escaping the mysterious Mister Oz's prison, Mr. Mxyzptlk conceals himself on Earth, disguised very convincingly as Clark Kent. Mxy is furious at Superman for failing to rescue him from Mister Oz, so he kidnaps the Man of Steel's son—Jon. Lois Lane and Superman go after him, but Mxy's magic makes them forget that they are even a family. However, Jon is able to contact the essence of their former selves and force them to remember.

VITAL STATS

REAL NAME (Unpronounceable)

OCCUPATION Trickster

HEIGHT Variable

WEIGHT Variable

BASE Fifth Dimension

MAIN ALLIES Bat-Mite

MAIN FOES Superman, Lois Lane, Mister Oz

NEW CHALLENGERS
DEATH-DEFYING ADVENTURERS

Four ordinary people are plucked from the moment of their deaths and taken to Challengers Mountain, the hollowed-out headquarters of the Challengers. The four, all natural survivors with particular skill sets, are told that they are now part of a unique team that investigates the mysteries of the universe. Hourglass tattoos on their bodies represent the borrowed time they are living on. Once they leave the safety of the mountain, the hourglasses will start to run out.

MEMBERS INCLUDE

1. TRINA ALVAREZ Trina is a herbalist who wants to help people.

2. PROF Walter is a mysterious man who brings the team together.

3. KRUNCH This muscly hero provides the brute strength for the team.

4. BETHANY HOPKINS Bethany is very comfortable using firearms.

CHALLENGING THE CHALLENGERS

After the confusion, terror, and adrenaline of their first mission, the New Challengers return to Challengers Mountain to try to get some straight answers from Prof about what is going on. However, the new heroes are not the only ones with questions. Four men appear in the room and take down the Prof. They say that they are the original Challengers of the Unknown and want answers as well.

NEW GODS
WARRING IMMORTALS

The New Gods are the inhabitants of the twin worlds of New Genesis and Apokolips. They used to share the same planet, but a destructive war split them into two factions. The Gods of New Genesis, led by Highfather, are largely peaceful. However, those on Apokolips are twisted with anger and a desire for conquest, following the example of their ruler Darkseid.

MEMBERS INCLUDE

1. LIGHTRAY This New God can fly at the speed of light and has control over solar energy.

2. HIGHFATHER The ruler of New Genesis is also the brother of Darkseid.

3. METRON Metron is an explorer from New Genesis.

4. ORION Darkseid's son, Orion, is brought up on New Genesis.

5. BEKKA Bekka is a warrior, and she is also a goddess of love.

FALL OF THE OLD GODS

When life first appeared in the Multiverse, it was ruled over by the Old Gods. However, even these powerful beings were vulnerable to jealousy and pride. They fought among themselves and returned to dust. From that dust, the New Gods were created. They initially lived in peace, but darkness had also been reborn in the form of Darkseid. A war between Darkseid and his brother Highfather left their world devastated, and the pair parted to rule the separate worlds of New Genesis and Apokolips.

NIGHTWING
ROBIN GROWN

Having learned the art of crime fighting from Batman, Dick Grayson leaves the identity of Robin behind and becomes Nightwing. Although he shares many of Batman's skills and traits, Nightwing is more outgoing, making friends everywhere he goes. He is a natural team player and leader, as well as being one of the most outstanding acrobats in the world.

POWERS

Nightwing may lack superpowers, but he has had a lifetime of training, first in acrobatics at Haly's Circus and then in combat and detective skills under Batman. Like Batman, he is an expert in disguise, and he also has valuable espionage experience from his time as an agent of the Spyral organization.

Nightwing's mask conceals his identity and is shaped like his Wingding weapons

VITAL STATS

REAL NAME Richard "Dick" Grayson

OCCUPATION Vigilante

HEIGHT 5 ft 10 in (1.78 m)

WEIGHT 175 lb. (79 kg)

BASE New York City; Blüdhaven

MAIN ALLIES Titans, The Bat-Family, Justice League

MAIN FOES The Joker, Two-Face, Deathstroke

Suit gives extra protection and stores an assortment of weapons, including Nightwing's version of Batarangs—Wingdings

NEW BEGINNINGS

When Doctor Destiny tries to steal information from Nightwing's mind through his dreams, Superman steps in to help. This Superman is actually from an alternate universe, but he has an instant affinity for Grayson, as he was friends with the one in his own universe. Reminding Nightwing that he can always count on his many friends, Superman also suggests that Dick visit the city of Blüdhaven to become its protector.

NUIDIS VULKO

ATLANTEAN SCHEMER

Nuidis Vulko is an Atlantean and a former advisor to the rulers of the undersea kingdom. He masterfully manipulates Atlantean politics from behind the scenes. Vulko's loyalty to Atlantis causes him to make some questionable choices and ends up pitting him against Aquaman, the king he claims to support.

VITAL STATS

REAL NAME Nuidis Vulko

OCCUPATION Royal advisor

HEIGHT 5 ft 8 in (1.73 m)

WEIGHT 191 lb (87 kg)

BASE Atlantis

MAIN ALLIES Black Manta, Undercurrent

MAIN FOES Aquaman, Orm

Vulko is the first to admit that he is not a warrior, so his physique is not muscled like Aquaman's

POWERS

As an Atlantean, Vulko can live underwater indefinitely. He has extensive knowledge of Atlantean history and mythology. Vulko is a cunning political schemer who always claims his manipulations are for the betterment of Atlantis.

NULL AND VOID

Vulko joins the Undercurrent, a movement led by Aquaman trying to overthrow the tyrant king of Atlantis, Corum Rath. When Rath uses the power of the Abyssal Dark to become a monster, Vulko uses his extensive knowledge to seek help from an unusual source. He summons the spectral guardians of Atlantis, led by Elder Null, hoping that their power will be enough to defeat Rath.

Orm, a.k.a. Ocean Master, is Aquaman's half brother. He jealously plots to overthrow Aquaman, who is the rightful king of Atlantis. Orm is thrown in jail after an attempt to invade the surface world fails. When he gets out, Orm is conflicted about his brother, realizing that the safety of Atlantis is more important than family rivalry.

POWERS

Like his fellow Atlanteans, Ocean Master has superhuman levels of strength, speed, and durability. He is totally at home in the sea, able to breathe in it indefinitely and withstand high pressure. His senses are evolved to be able to see and hear even in the deep ocean. Ocean Master's weapon of choice is a trident.

His crown allows Ocean Master to control water

A NEW LIFE

Orm saves the life of a human named Erin and her young son, Tommy. He falls in love with Erin and decides to give up being Ocean Master, making a fresh start on dry land. Although he loves his new life, Orm becomes Ocean Master once more to try to stop a civil war in Atlantis.

Trident conjures up storms and fires lightning blasts

VITAL STATS

REAL NAME Orm

OCCUPATION Reformed super-villain

HEIGHT 5 ft 11 in (1.80 m)

WEIGHT 200 lb (91 kg)

BASE Holly Beach, Louisiana

MAIN ALLIES Tula, Black Manta, Lex Luthor

MAIN FOES Aquaman, Mera

OMAC
ONE-MAN ARMY CORPS

The sentient satellite Brother Eye infects scientist Kevin Kho with a virus. Now whenever Brother Eye wishes, he can turn Kevin into a living weapon named **OMAC** that he controls. OMAC is the perfect blend of biology and technology. He is also a brute, super-strong, and unable to speak more than a few words at a time.

One of OMAC's most distinctive features is his Mohawk fin

VITAL STATS

REAL NAME Kevin Kho

OCCUPATION Scientist

HEIGHT Variable

WEIGHT Variable

BASE Metropolis

MAIN ALLIES Blue Beetle, Project Cadmus

MAIN FOES Max Lord

POWERS

When Brother Eye triggers the "Omactivation," Kevin Kho becomes OMAC. In this form, he is super-strong and durable and can fire powerful energy beams. OMAC's powers can get out of control, and he is prone to going on rampages.

OMAC ARMY

With Kevin Kho defeated, Brother Eye is harnessed by the Colony, an organization looking to end crime in Gotham City. They use Brother Eye to convert their foot soldiers into an army of OMACs, who are then sent to attack and assimilate the Bat-Family. However, Bat-Family member Spoiler manages to break Red Robin free of Brother Eye and liberate the soldiers.

As OMAC, Kevin's size and strength are vastly increased

ORION
DOG OF WAR

Orion is the son of the tyrant Darkseid, sent to live with Highfather as part of a peace agreement between the planets Apokolips and New Genesis. Despite his evil father, Orion is welcomed to New Genesis and raised there like Highfather's true son. Orion is usually a good guy but is sometimes troubled by the darker, Apokoliptian parts of his nature.

Sunlike symbol on Orion's trademark helmet represents the New Gods

POWERS

Orion is a New God, which means he has super-strength, speed, and invulnerability. Under Highfather's guidance, he learns to control his fierce Apokoliptian temper. Orion is a formidable warrior, nicknamed the Dog of War, and a natural leader. His Mother Box allows him to locate anyone in the universe.

MAGNIFICENT MACHINE

Orion's favorite mode of transportation is his A4 Astro Harness. On it, he can call up "Boom Tube" portals to travel anywhere in the universe or fire concentrated energy blasts at enemies. It is also incredibly quick, as Orion demonstrates when he arrives just in time to help Wonder Woman escape the god Hermes.

VITAL STATS

REAL NAME Orion
OCCUPATION New God
HEIGHT 6 ft 1 in (1.85 m)
WEIGHT 195 lb (88 kg)
BASE New Genesis
MAIN ALLIES New Gods, Milan, the Amazons
MAIN FOES Darkseid, First Born

ORPHAN
ASSASSINS' DAUGHTER

The child of deadly assassins Lady Shiva and David Cain, Cassandra Cain adopts her father's code name after his death. Although she has been brought up to be a killer, Cassandra chooses a different path. She joins the team of young heroes that Batman and Batwoman are training to protect Gotham City.

Dark suit helps Orphan blend into the shadows

LIVING WEAPON

Told from birth she exists only to bring death, Cassandra realizes that she has the power to choose who she is when her friends are captured by Lady Shiva. Cassandra uses all her dark skills to rescue them, fighting her way through hordes of assassins before confronting Shiva, her estranged mother.

Orphan wears a Utility Belt like other Batman allies

POWERS

Cassandra is trained to read body language to figure out her opponents' weaknesses. She is one of the world's finest martial artists, capable of taking on multiple foes at one time. She is also highly skilled in the use of weapons such as Batarangs.

VITAL STATS

REAL NAME Cassandra Cain
OCCUPATION Vigilante
HEIGHT 5 ft 5 in (1.65 m)
WEIGHT 110 lb (50 kg)
BASE Gotham City
MAIN ALLIES The Bat-Family, The Gotham Knights
MAIN FOES Lady Shiva

PARALLAX
FEAR ENTITY

Parallax is the living embodiment of the emotion of fear and possesses the bodies of others. For a long time, he is imprisoned in the Central Power Battery of the Green Lantern Corps, but he is freed by Sinestro. Unlike beings previously possessed by Parallax, Sinestro manages to control him and channel his power, before his hold is broken by Green Lantern Hal Jordan.

Parallax has no fixed appearance but usually appears in the form of a giant monster

POWERS

Parallax has similar, but greater, powers to a member of the Sinestro Corps, creating hard-light constructs in yellow. He can also control the minds of others and force them to feel fear. Parallax can assume any shape he chooses, usually something that will be scary to opponents.

Parallax is always yellow, the color of fear on the emotional spectrum

MAN OF FEAR

Parallax lures Superman to him by kidnapping children and then possesses the hero. The Parallax-controlled Superman attracts Sinestro's attention, who takes him to the planet Qward. Here Superman reveals that he allowed Parallax to possess him to save the children. Superman senses that Parallax is desperate to avoid being controlled by Sinestro again, so he imprisons him in Sinestro's power ring and gives it to the Green Lantern Corps for safekeeping.

PARASITE
POWER ABSORBER

Bike courier Joshua Michael Allen is already having a bad day when he runs into a huge, bloblike alien in the streets of Metropolis. The encounter turns Joshua into Parasite, an always-hungry creature capable of consuming metahuman powers and then using them himself. Unfortunately, the powers that Parasite likes the taste of most of all are Superman's.

Parasite no longer has human jaws but instead has a mouth resembling a giant leech's

VITAL STATS

REAL NAME Joshua Michael Allen

OCCUPATION Super-villain

HEIGHT 6 ft 6 in (1.98 m)

WEIGHT 267 lb (121 kg)

BASE Belle Reve Penitentiary

MAIN ALLIES Suicide Squad (Task Force XL)

MAIN FOES Superman

POWERS

Parasite is able to feed on the abilities of metahumans. When he does this, he is able to use their powers for a short time. This means that when fighting Superman, Parasite is in theory evenly matched with the Man of Steel. However, Parasite cannot always master his new powers and can be outwitted.

OVEREATING

Lois Lane is knocked unconscious from absorbing Brainiac's psychic abilities, and Parasite cannot resist coming to feed off her new powers. Superman fights the villain off, but he realizes that maybe Parasite can cure Lois. The Man of Steel lets Parasite absorb Lois's powers, and she wakes from her coma, while the villain is knocked out, overloaded by the massive power feast.

Parasite's body can increase in size when he absorbs new powers

THE PENGUIN
GENTLEMAN OF CRIME

With a talent for crime and a fondness for birds, the Penguin rules Gotham City's criminal underworld with an iron ... umbrella. This has brought him into conflict with Batman, although, unlike most of the hero's foes, the Penguin is perfectly sane. He conducts his slippery criminal activities from his nightclub, the Iceberg Lounge. There is little that goes on in Gotham City without the Penguin's knowledge.

The Penguin is always turned out smartly in an old-fashioned gentleman's suit, top hat, and monocle

VOTE PENGUIN!

When the Gotham City district of Burnside is hit by a blizzard, the Penguin arrives to help the citizens cope. Batgirl is suspicious, and discovers that the villain is hatching a plot to run for US Congress. He is even using a gadget stolen by his son to make people trust him. The Penguin is furious that he has been exposed and shows his true colors by berating his son for failing him.

POWERS

What he lacks in stature—and superpowers—the Penguin makes up for in pure cunning. He is a clever strategist who has plotted his way to the top of the criminal underworld in Gotham City. Despite his appearance, the Penguin can hold his own in a fight and is adept at handling his weaponized umbrellas.

PHANTOM GIRL
INTANGIBLE TOUCH

Like all beings of the planet Bgztl, Linnya Wazzo has the natural ability to render herself in a ghostlike, intangible form. Linnya is trapped alone in the Dark Multiverse as a child. She is discovered years later by Mister Terrific, Plastic Man, and Metamorpho, joining them when they return to Earth. The foursome discover they share a lingering dark energy bond that forces them to stay in close proximity—or risk being destroyed.

VITAL STATS

REAL NAME Linnya Wazzo

OCCUPATION Super Hero

HEIGHT 5 ft 4 in (1.63 m)

WEIGHT 106 lb (48 kg)

BASE Mobile

MAIN ALLIES The Terrifics

MAIN FOES None

As a member of the new Terrifics team, Phantom Girl adds a "T" symbol to her costume

POWERS

In her intangible form, Phantom Girl can pass through solid objects, is invulnerable, and does not need to eat. However, on Earth she discovers that, in her solid form, anything she touches explodes!

GOING HOME

Linnya has not seen her home planet for many years, so Mister Terrific agrees to take her there. But what he hasn't told her is that what felt like 10 years to her in the Dark Multiverse was actually 32 years on Bgztl. Linnya is shocked to see that her mother is now an elderly woman, but the two share a long-awaited embrace.

Natives of Bgztl prefer to wear black and white, and the Terrifics follows this color scheme for its uniforms

PHANTOM STRANGER
REDEMPTION SEEKER

Judas Iscariot is deemed one of the three worst sinners in the world, so he is given the robe of the friend he betrayed and condemned to walk the Earth for eternity. Known only as the Phantom Stranger, he looks for people to help, hoping that one day his sins will be forgiven.

POWERS

The immortal Phantom Stranger's powers are mysterious and may be without limit. He can pause time so that he can accomplish his missions without disrupting the world around him. He can teleport, change size, and become invisible. The Stranger can fire powerful energy blasts and possesses a great deal of knowledge about others.

INTO THE AFTERLIFE

Batman recruits the Phantom Stranger for a mission to the afterlife to find Doctor Light and clear Superman's name. Although at first the Stranger refuses, his heart is touched when he finds out that Light has left a wife and children. The Stranger and Batman—accompanied by Deadman and Katana—find Doctor Light but are stopped from bringing him back to life by the angel Zauriel.

The Phantom Stranger's trademark hat conceals his face in shadow

Eyes appear pupilless and totally white

VITAL STATS

REAL NAME Judas Iscariot

OCCUPATION Wanderer

HEIGHT 6 ft 2 in (1.88 m)

WEIGHT 185 lb (84 kg)

BASE Mobile

MAIN ALLIES Council of Immortals, Trinity of Sin, Justice League Dark

MAIN FOES The Spectre, Trigon, Sin Eater

PLASTIC MAN
THE POWER OF STRETCH

Petty thief Patrick "Eel" O'Brian is given incredible elastic powers when he gets covered in a mysterious chemical. However, rather than using his new abilities to further his criminal career, he becomes a Super Hero. As Plastic Man, he brings an unusual skill set to missions—and a good supply of wisecracks to keep up morale!

VITAL STATS

REAL NAME Patrick "Eel" O'Brian

OCCUPATION Super Hero

HEIGHT 6 ft 1 in (1.85 m)

WEIGHT 178 lb (81 kg)

BASE Chicago

MAIN ALLIES Justice League, The Terrifics

MAIN FOES None

White-framed shades help conceal Plastic Man's identity, while also making a style statement!

PLASTIC FANTASTIC

While trapped in the Dark Multiverse, Plastic Man discovers that he is a conductor for all its negative cosmic energies. He withdraws into an egg-shaped cocoon to stop himself from losing control. But when his allies beg him for help battling the dark minions of the demon Barbatos, he bursts out of his shell in all kinds of giant, bizarre shapes.

Plastic Man's color scheme evolves from red and yellow to black and white when he joins the Terrifics team

POWERS

Plastic Man can alter the shape and size of his body in almost any way imaginable. This makes him almost invulnerable to conventional weapons—only sudden, intense heat or cold is a threat to him, as it can cause him to melt or freeze solid. Even then, his ability to regenerate means he can survive being shattered into microscopic pieces.

POISON IVY
QUEEN OF GREEN

After botanist Pamela Isley is doused in a plant serum she creates, she gains superpowers and turns into Poison Ivy. Ivy is an eco-terrorist who has control over plants and places their rights above those of humans. Through her powers, she has a connection to the Green, the elemental force connecting all plant life on the planet.

Poison Ivy's preferred method of transferring toxins to her enemies is via a kiss

POWERS

Ivy's exposure to her own plant serum makes her immune to all poisons and toxins. However, she can poison others with a touch. Ivy can also release chemicals that make people do as she wants, particularly men. She can control plants, making them grow and twist rapidly to ensnare her opponents.

VITAL STATS

REAL NAME Pamela Isley

OCCUPATION Scientist, eco-terrorist

HEIGHT 5 ft 8 in (1.73 m)

WEIGHT 115 lb (52 kg)

BASE Gotham City

MAIN ALLIES Harley Quinn, Birds of Prey, the Green

MAIN FOES Batman, The Joker

EVERYONE LOVES IVY

Ivy decides that the world would be a better place if she controlled it, so she puts a potion in the plants that people eat. Soon she controls everyone on the planet, and the only ones immune to her charm are Catwoman and Batman, who have taken an antidote. Batman manages to release Ivy's close friend Harley Quinn, who makes Ivy see reason.

POWER GIRL
HERO OF EARTH-2

Kara is Earth-2's equivalent of Supergirl. The cousin of her Earth's Superman, she is raised by him and his wife, Lois Lane. After her Earth and its heroes are devastated by the forces of Darkseid, Power Girl escapes to Prime Earth. Here she continues to be a Super Hero, although she is always looking for a way to get home.

In common with Prime Earth's Superman and Supergirl, Power Girl wears a red cape

POWERS

As a Kryptonian, Kara has a range of amazing superpowers when exposed to Earth's yellow sun, but is also vulnerable to magic and Kryptonite. She has heat and X-ray vision and freeze-breath, plus super-strength, speed, and durability. She also has super-breath, which allows her to exhale hurricane strength winds.

Power Girl does not wear the S-shield that other Superman Family members wear

TRAPPED

Returning to Earth-2 after a spell on Prime Earth, Power Girl transfers her powers to Tanya Spears, who becomes the new Power Girl. Later, Tanya dreams that the original Power Girl is trapped between dimensions. Tanya rigs up a machine that enables her to reach Kara, but when Tanya's physical body is disconnected from it, both Power Girls are left stranded.

VITAL STATS

REAL NAME Kara Zor-El

OCCUPATION Super Hero, businesswoman

HEIGHT 5 ft 11 in (1.80 m)

WEIGHT 180 lb (82 kg)

BASE Earth-2

MAIN ALLIES Justice Society of America, Huntress (Earth-2)

MAIN FOES Darkseid

PROFESSOR HUGO STRANGE
MAD SCIENTIST

Hugo Strange is an expert on madness and the human brain. He creates a growth serum that he uses to turn ordinary people into Monster Men—oversized brutes whom Strange can use to cause chaos in Gotham City. Strange's genius often tips into madness, thanks to his very unhealthy obsession with Batman.

STRANGE BATMAN

Strange creates Monster Men just to get the Dark Knight's attention. When Batman tracks him down, Strange is wearing his own Batsuit—rigged with explosives set to go off if the hero so much as touches him. Strange's plan is to kill the original Dark Knight and become Gotham City's new Batman, but the hero and his allies defeat him.

Professor Hugo Strange wears a distinctive pair of round spectacles

Strange is recognizable from his bald-headed but bearded look

VITAL STATS

REAL NAME Hugo Strange

OCCUPATION Psychologist

HEIGHT 5 ft 10 in (1.78 m)

WEIGHT 170 lb (77 kg)

BASE Gotham City

MAIN ALLIES Monster Men, Psycho-Pirate, Amanda Waller

MAIN FOES Batman, Nightwing

POWERS

Strange has no superpowers but does possess a genius-level intellect. His particular area of expertise is the brain and the way it functions. However, he is not just a brain; Strange has also honed his body to the peak of physical fitness.

PROMETHEUS
TECH REVOLUTIONARY

Prometheus blames the authorities for the loss of his parents, and dedicates his life to trying to bring them down—by any means necessary. He uses his genius to create a warsuit containing an artificial intelligence to give him the edge in battle. He also manages to forge a connection to the other-dimensional Ghost Zone.

VITAL STATS

REAL NAME Unknown

OCCUPATION Super-villain

HEIGHT 6 ft 1 in (1.85 m)

WEIGHT 180 lb (82 kg)

BASE The Ghost Zone

MAIN ALLIES Afterthought

MAIN FOES Justice League of America, Midnighter

POWERS

Prometheus trains his body and his mind to maximize his potential. His high-tech helmet's artificial intelligence devises ways to beat even strong opponents like the Justice League of America. He is also a master of disguise.

As well as providing protection, Prometheus's warsuit feeds him information to help him win fights

Prometheus fights using a nightstick that pulses with energy

SANCTUARY INVASION

The Justice League of America often lets members of the public into its Sanctuary headquarters. This allows Prometheus to enter the base in disguise as a documentary filmmaker. He soon reveals his plan to blow up the Sanctuary with the League and many innocent members of the public in it. However, Prometheus is overconfident, and the heroes manage to defeat him together.

RĀ'S AL GHŪL
THE DEMON'S HEAD

Rā's al Ghūl is determined to save Earth—even if it means destroying humanity to do it. He has spent centuries observing the negative impact of people on the planet and wants to restore the environment. He is one of Batman's most dangerous foes and the leader of the League of Assassins.

Rā's is one of the world's best swordsmen

HISTORY OF VIOLENCE

Rā's al Ghūl has spent centuries formulating plans and spreading devastation to achieve his evil goal. He is known to have caused the Great Fire of London in 1666; the New York City cholera outbreak of 1832; and World War I in 1914.

Rā's servants and bodyguards are always called Ubu

POWERS

Rā's al Ghūl has mastered the Lazarus Pits, giving him virtual immortality as long as he has access to them. Repeated use of the pits has also given him enhanced strength, stamina, and durability. He is a genius, a master strategist, and one of the few people to have worked out Batman's secret identity.

RAVAGER
DEATHSTROKE'S DAUGHTER

Rose Wilson, a.k.a. Ravager, is the daughter of the lethal assassin Deathstroke. Although she inherits his abilities and natural aptitude for combat, Deathstroke tries to stop Rose turning out like him. He makes a deal with Dick Grayson that he will stop attacking the Teen Titans if Dick trains Rose, so she learns Robin's values instead of his own.

Like her father, Deathstroke, Ravager has silver hair

FAMILY BUSINESS

Deathstroke decides to stop being a villain and forms a team, code named Defiance, to do good. He recruits Rose to be a part of it. While the two have a difficult relationship, as Deathstroke does with all his children, Rose sees Defiance as an opportunity to be a hero. She wields an energy staff instead of her usual sword when fighting with Defiance.

POWERS

Ravager is sometimes able to see visions of her immediate future, enabling her to avert danger if needed. However, she is also ready to face danger head on, with her sword and martial arts skills. She also has superhuman strength, stamina, speed, and reflexes, plus an advanced healing factor, all inherited from Deathstroke.

Ravager's sword is made from inertron, a near-indestructible metal found only in the future

VITAL STATS

REAL NAME Rose Wilson
OCCUPATION Mercenary
HEIGHT 5 ft 4 in (1.63 m)
WEIGHT 116 lb (53 kg)
BASE Mobile
MAIN ALLIES Hosun, Wintergreen, Nightwing
MAIN FOES None

RAVEN
DAUGHTER OF EVIL

Raven is half-human and half-demon, the daughter of the evil Trigon. She decides to choose a heroic path but is locked in a constant struggle with the demonic side of her nature, which sometimes threatens to break through. After a lifetime of not fitting in, Raven finally finds a home, first with the Teen Titans and then later the Titans.

Secretive by nature, Raven often partially hides her face with her hood

Raven sometimes wears clawed gloves, mimicking the claws of a real raven

POWERS

Raven can project a Soul-Self, an astral form that enables her to observe distant people and events, or even attack enemies. She also has a range of powerful psychic abilities, like mind-reading, sensing emotions, and even altering memories. Raven can also teleport, fly, and use a range of magic spells.

JOURNEY INTO THE PAST

Confronting a man who has been watching her, Raven is pushed into his fireplace ... and finds herself in San Francisco in 1906. A massive earthquake is devastating the city and causing many casualties. Raven uses her powers to do what she can, saving lives and healing the injured. Amid the rubble, Raven is inspired by the ordinary people helping each other.

VITAL STATS

REAL NAME Rachel Roth

OCCUPATION Super Hero

HEIGHT 5 ft 11 in (1.80 m)

WEIGHT 139 lb (63 kg)

BASE Hall of Justice

MAIN ALLIES Titans, Teen Titans

MAIN FOES Trigon

THE RAY
NIGHT BOY

Ray Terrill's childhood is spent indoors, since his mother thinks he is allergic to light. When the story reaches the media, he becomes known as the Night Boy. The truth is very different—light gives Ray superpowers. Ray finally goes out into the world and realizes that his powers could make him a hero, just like the ones he used to watch on TV.

Ray's helmet is a hard-light construct he created himself

When using his powers, the Ray normally appears almost entirely black, except his eyes and the gold details on his costume

VITAL STATS

REAL NAME Raymond Terrill

OCCUPATION Super Hero

HEIGHT 5 ft 10 in (1.85 m)

WEIGHT 155 lb (70 kg)

BASE Vanity, Oregon

MAIN ALLIES Justice League of America

MAIN FOES Sons of Liberty

POWERS

The Ray can absorb light and then use it in a variety of ways. He can create hard-light constructs, make himself invisible, and fire out light blasts. He can also move at the speed of light and use his stored energy to fly. By turning into a being of pure energy, the Ray can heal any wound that he suffers.

CASTLE OF LIGHT

The Justice League of America is chasing the villain Chronos through time to stop him from killing the God of Super Heroes. Chronos assembles an army of soldiers taken from throughout history, but the Ray has an idea for slowing them down. Using all his strength, the Ray creates his largest ever hologram—a castle made entirely of hard light.

RED ARROW

Emiko Queen is Green Arrow's half-sister. They have the same father but Emiko's mother is the assassin Shado. Emiko is a skilled archer and martial artist and at first is an enemy to Green Arrow before realizing that she wants to be a hero like him. She adopts the code name Red Arrow, and Green Arrow accepts her as a comrade.

VITAL STATS

REAL NAME Emiko "Emi" Queen

OCCUPATION Super Hero

HEIGHT 5 ft 2 in (1.57 m)

WEIGHT 100 lb (45 kg)

BASE Seattle, WA

MAIN ALLIES Teen Titans, Team Arrow

MAIN FOES Ninth Circle

Red Arrow wears a hood like Green Arrow

BLOOD TIES

Team Arrow members all have difficult home lives, which is why they all stick together in their Arrow family. When Green Arrow's mother tries to shoot him with an arrow, it is Emi who throws herself in its path. Green Arrow fears the worst, but Emi is made of tough stuff, and recovers in tho hocpital. Hor big brothor rewards her by finally using her code name—Red Arrow.

POWERS

Like her brother, Emi is an incredibly talented archer, and Green Arrow believes she may even be better than him. She was also raised to be an assassin, training in combat and stealth techniques. Emi's acrobatic ability is so heightened that she can even dodge bullets.

RED HOOD
ROBIN REBORN

Jason Todd is a former Robin, killed by The Joker but brought back to life by a Lazarus Pit. This resurrected hero has a slightly different attitude toward crime fighting than his former mentor Batman and adopts a strategy of posing as a bad guy while really being a good guy. Now known as Red Hood, he leads a team called the Outlaws.

Red Hood's mask is thought to have been worn by The Joker, before he became The Joker

This red chest symbol is also equipped with a taser to shock opponents

POWERS

Since his training with Talia al Ghūl and the League of Assassins, Red Hood is a supreme martial artist and swordsman. He can also summon the All-Blades with the force of his will. These weapons, a gift from the Assassins' Guild after he came back from the dead, work against magic-powered enemies.

DEEP UNDER COVER

Red Hood wants to be the hero who can go to places that Batman can't. After his resurrection in a Lazarus Pit, Jason returns to Gotham City to infiltrate the Black Mask operation by posing as a criminal. Red Hood has to look convincing, so he attacks the Mayor, bringing him into conflict with his former mentor Batman.

VITAL STATS

REAL NAME Jason Todd

OCCUPATION Vigilante

HEIGHT 6 ft (1.83 m)

WEIGHT 225 lb (102 kg)

BASE Gotham City

MAIN ALLIES The Outlaws, the Bat-Family, Arsenal

MAIN FOES The Joker

RED ROBIN
BATMAN'S DETECTIVE HEIR

Tim Drake is a young man with an incredible investigative mind. He impresses Batman by deducing not only his secret identity but also those of Dick Grayson and Jason Todd. Tim trains under Batman as the new hero Red Robin and brings a fine analytical mind and technological capabilities to the fight against crime in Gotham City.

POWERS

Red Robin has no superpowers, but he has extensive training under the watchful eye of Batman. He is an accomplished martial artist. Red Robin's biggest assets are his detective skills—which perhaps even surpass those of the Dark Knight himself. He has a genius-level intellect and is a computer-hacking expert.

Red Robin's "RR" symbol and costume are an evolution of his old Robin suit

A NEW PATH

After escaping the clutches of Mister Oz, Tim discovers a possible future in which he becomes Batman. He decides to learn more about alternate timelines. Telling Batman that he is going to Ivy University, Tim instead hits the road with his girlfriend Stephanie Brown, a.k.a. Spoiler, to see what they can learn about the Multiverse.

VITAL STATS

REAL NAME Timothy Jackson "Tim" Drake

OCCUPATION Crime fighter

HEIGHT 5 ft 6 in (1.68 m)

WEIGHT 125 lb (57 kg)

BASE Gotham City

MAIN ALLIES Batman, Teen Titans The Gotham Knights,

MAIN FOES The Joker, The Colony

Red Robin carries his own set of Batarangs

RED TORNADO
ANDROID WHIRLWIND

Created by Dr. T. O. Morrow, Red Tornado is an extremely intelligent sentient android. Red Tornado is self-aware enough to decide for himself to be a hero. He has the ability to use his body to summon powerful winds. Red Tornado joins the Challengers of the Unknown's investigations into the rare Nth Metal.

One of Red Tornado's most distinguishing features is the yellow arrow on his forehead

POWERS

Red Tornado is built to have super-strength and durability. He is also super-intelligent. He can use his arms and his body to create powerful whirlwinds. His powers create wind harmonics, which can be traced to discover where he has been.

VITAL STATS

REAL NAME None

OCCUPATION Android

HEIGHT 6 ft 1 in (1.85 m)

WEIGHT 325 lb (147 kg)

BASE Blackhawk Island

MAIN ALLIES T. O. Morrow, Metal Men

MAIN FOES Barbatos

HARBINGER OF DOOM

Red Tornado returns from the center of the Multiverse to warn Earth's heroes that the demon Barbatos is coming. The Flash (Barry Allen), Cyborg, and Raven try to reach the Multiverse's center by tracing the path left by Red Tornado. But it is a trap, laid by Barbatos, to use the heroes' ship to destroy the Multiverse. Red Tornado is so convinced that all is lost that he turns his fear switch to "off."

RENEE MONTOYA

TO SERVE AND PROTECT

Renee Montoya trains as a detective under Harvey Bullock at the Gotham City Police Department before moving to Blüdhaven Police Department. However, she returns to Gotham City to join the task force backing up Commissioner Gordon while he is standing in for the Dark Knight. There is no question that Renee is a brave cop and a good person, who hates corruption.

As a detective, Montoya does not have to wear a GCPD uniform

POWERS

As a trained police officer, Renee Montoya is skilled in the use of firearms and basic hand-to-hand combat. She is also a GCPD detective so has advanced investigative skills. Renee is brave, and willing to fight against great odds to serve and protect Gotham City.

DAUGHTERS OF GOTHAM

When a virus is released targeting only Gotham City's men, Renee is left very short-staffed at the Police Department. At least crime is down 90 percent! A group calling itself the Daughters of Gotham is responsible for the outbreak, and Montoya teams up with female Super Heroes from Gotham City and beyond, plus a few female villains, to stop them.

VITAL STATS

REAL NAME Renee Montoya

OCCUPATION Police detective

HEIGHT 5 ft 8 in (1.73 m)

WEIGHT 144 lb (65 kg)

BASE Gotham City

MAIN ALLIES Commissioner Jim Gordon, Detective Harvey Bullock, Batwoman

MAIN FOES Daughters of Gotham, Nancy Yip

REVERSE-FLASH
NUMBER-ONE FAN

Eobard Thawne is the biggest fan of The Flash (Barry Allen) in Central City in the 25th century. But when Barry travels to the future and Thawne finally meets his hero, he is angry that Barry treats him just like everybody else. Thawne vows revenge; he gains Speed Force powers from an old The Flash suit in a time capsule and becomes the evil Reverse-Flash.

Reverse-Flash's Negative Speed Force powers manifest as red lightning

VITAL STATS

REAL NAME Eobard Thawne

OCCUPATION Super-villain, former museum curator

HEIGHT 5 ft 11 in (1.80 m)

WEIGHT 179 lb (81 kg)

BASE Central City

MAIN ALLIES Secret Society of Super-Villains

MAIN FOES The Flash Family

Reverse-Flash's suit uses the same colors as The Flash's but swapped around

REVERSE-FLASH VS. BATMAN

Back in the 21st century, Reverse-Flash is hit by a lightning strike that restores a memory of a past defeat at the hands of Batman. Reverse-Flash heads to the Batcave, where he surprises and attacks Batman, who is waiting for The Flash (Barry Allen).

POWERS

Reverse-Flash's manipulation of the Speed Force gives him speedster powers—he is in fact even faster than The Flash (Barry Allen)—and enables him to travel through time. He is extremely strong and has incredible reflexes and agility. Reverse-Flash's body can regenerate from even the most terrible wounds, and his control of time effectively makes him immortal.

RICK FLAG
SUICIDE SQUAD COMMANDER

Like his father and grandfather before him, Rick Flag serves in the military with distinction and courage. But he is put in prison when he refuses an order that will endanger the lives of his unit. Flag is then recruited by Amanda Waller to command the Suicide Squad. He keeps his criminal teammates in line and focused on their missions.

Flag is an expert in all types of firearms

POWERS

Rick Flag is not a metahuman, but he is a former US Navy SEAL with expertise in weapons, tactics, and leadership. He always tries to do the right thing and tries to protect those under his command no matter the cost.

Belt is specially designed to hold ammunition

RETURNING HERO

Rick Flag heroically traps himself inside the Phantom Zone, an interdimensional prison, to stop an army of Kryptonian criminals invading Earth. Later, his Suicide Squad teammates also get sucked into the Phantom Zone. Flag is able to bring all of them out safely using a special space suit given to him by his long-lost grandfather.

VITAL STATS

REAL NAME Richard Flag Jr.

OCCUPATION Soldier

HEIGHT 6 ft 1 in (1.85 m)

WEIGHT 189 lb (86 kg)

BASE Washington, D.C.

MAIN ALLIES Suicide Squad, The Wall

MAIN FOES Annihilation Brigade, General Zod

THE RIDDLER
ENIGMATIC VILLAIN

The Riddler gets his super-villain identity from his love of creating and solving puzzles. He leaves riddles at all of his crime scenes in Gotham City, challenging Batman to solve them—which the Dark Knight usually does. The Riddler is frequently locked up in Arkham Asylum, although he claims to know a variety of ways to escape if he ever wants to.

VITAL STATS

REAL NAME Edward Nygma
OCCUPATION Criminal
HEIGHT 6 ft 1 in (1.85 m)
WEIGHT 183 lb (83 kg)
BASE Gotham City
MAIN ALLIES None
MAIN FOES Batman, Robin, The Joker

Bowler hat in the Riddler's favorite colors, purple and green

RIDDLER'S LABYRINTH

After the Batman Who Laughs invades Gotham City from the Dark Multiverse, he frees the Riddler from Arkham Asylum. The Riddler is given the task of guarding the first section of a labyrinth designed to trap heroes trying to free the city. Although Harley Quinn and Killer Croc fail to solve his riddle, the villain is defeated when boy genius Robin shows up.

Cufflinks with the Riddler's question mark symbol

POWERS

Edward Nygma is a genius, able to craft complex traps, puzzles, and weapons. This includes his main weapon, a staff shaped like a question mark. It can be customized to be a remote control for other weapons, electrified, or even turned into a firearm.

RIP HUNTER
TIME MASTER

Rip Hunter uses his extensive knowledge of time travel to become a Time Master. These brave heroes protect others from villains who use time travel for evil purposes. He is the son of fellow time traveler Booster Gold, but he keeps the details of his life secret so that his foes cannot trace him in the timestream.

Rip Hunter's suit is mainly in his favorite color—green

POWERS

Rip does not have superpowers but describes himself as a "next-level science genius." His greatest invention is the Time Sphere, which he uses to travel almost anywhere in the past or future. Although not a fighter by nature, Hunter knows various combat techniques to use in dangerous situations.

VITAL STATS

REAL NAME Unknown

OCCUPATION Time traveler

HEIGHT 5 ft 11 in (1.80 m)

WEIGHT 175 lb (79 kg)

BASE Mobile

MAIN ALLIES Time Masters, Booster Gold, Goldstar

MAIN FOES Deimos, Sarko

Rip carries a device with him that lets him check how the timeline is affected by the actions of himself and others

ONE DAY TO SAVE THE FUTURE

Rip warns the Green Lantern Corps that it will be destroyed in the future if it does not act now. He is pursuing a being named Sarko, who hates the Corps and is planning to kill all of its members using the powerful weapon named Krona's Gauntlet. Green Lantern Hal Jordan takes Rip to find Sarko and destroys the Gauntlet, saving the future of the Corps.

ROBIN
SON OF BATMAN

Damian Wayne is Bruce Wayne's son. Although he started life as an assassin-in-training with his mother, Talia al Ghūl, Damian is now a Super Hero. Damian is the latest to hold the Robin code name and leads the Teen Titans. Despite his young age, Damian is an expert fighter and a genius, but his ego sometimes runs away with him.

Black hood is a legacy from his time as an assassin

Green mask disguises his identity

POWERS

Damian is extremely talented and intelligent, having spent most of his childhood in training. First he learns the skills of an assassin with his mother, then later is taught crime-fighting subjects—like forensics, escapology, and disguise—by Batman.

THE DEMON'S FAMILY

Damian's grandfather is the super-villain Rā's al Ghūl—leader of the League of Assassins. The boy is brought up in this family's dubious traditions, leading a school of young assassins named the Demon's Fist. However, as he gets older, Damian turns his back on Rā's and follows instead in his father's footsteps.

VITAL STATS

REAL NAME Damian Wayne

OCCUPATION Student, Super Hero

HEIGHT 5 ft 4 in (1.63 m)

WEIGHT 84 lb (38 kg)

BASE Gotham City

MAIN ALLIES Batman, Superboy, Teen Titans

MAIN FOES League of Assassins, Heretic

SATURN GIRL
TELEPATH FROM TITAN

Saturn Girl originally comes from Titan, a moon of Saturn, in the 31st century. She is a powerful telepath, and a founding member and sometimes leader of the Legion of Super-Heroes. Saturn Girl will always put herself in danger if it means saving another life. She is romantically involved with her teammate Lightning Lad.

Powerful Legion Flight Ring is given to all Legionnaires

Silhouette of the ringed planet she is named after

ARKHAM INMATE

After Saturn Girl arrives in the 21st century, she steals some food and winds up at the police station. She explains to the puzzled detectives that food is free where she comes from, and adds that she's seen the future. They don't believe her, and she ends up in Arkham Asylum. Here she helps Reggie Long, a.k.a. Rorschach, escape, and the two go on to help the elderly Johnny Thunder of the Justice Society.

POWERS

Saturn Girl is a skilled telepath, an ability common among those from Titan. She can read the minds of others, communicate with them, and control them if necessary. Thanks to her Legion Flight Ring, she can fly safely through space.

SCARECROW
MASTER OF FEAR

Having suffered a traumatic childhood, Jonathan Crane grows up to become a leading expert on phobias. His obsession with studying and controlling fear leads him into becoming the weird and terrifying Scarecrow, giving the citizens of Gotham City waking nightmares with his fear toxin.

Signature burlap mask is intended to make Scarecrow more terrifying

YELLOW LANTERN

Scarecrow is chosen by a yellow power ring to become a Yellow Lantern and spread pure ter[...]. He studies the [...] and works out how to harness its powe[...] to create fear. Crane embeds fear energy into a viral video to make people scared of Batman. With help from the Green Lanterns, Batman takes down Scarecrow.

VITAL STATS

REAL NAME Jonathan Crane

OCCUPATION Scientist, super-villain

HEIGHT 6 ft (1.83 m)

WEIGHT 210 lb (91 kg)

BASE Gotham City

MAIN ALLIES Secret Society of Super-Villains

MAIN FOES Batman, Robin, Batwoman

POWERS

Scarecrow has no superpowers but is a genius scientist, inventing a toxin that can cause people to experience their greatest fears. Although this is his main weapon, the gangly Crane also comes up with his own unique style of kung fu.

Franklin Rock is a Pittsburgh steelworker when he is called upon to serve his country in World War II. As a member of the legendary Easy Company, Sergeant Rock takes part in the battle for Normandy in 1944, as well as several other missions. Sergeant Rock serves with distinction and is awarded the Distinguished Service Cross.

Rock wears his sergeant rank insignia on his helmet

POWERS

Sergeant Rock is an elite infantryman who has deadly accuracy with a firearm. He is also an expert in close combat. Rock is protective of the men under his command and never falters in following his missions to the end.

Rock always carries a .50 caliber ammo belt for luck, even though he carries no weapon that uses that type of ammunition

STRANGE ALLEGIANCES

Sergeant Rock is fighting to liberate a small French town in 1944 when he and Easy Company get trapped in a time bubble, along with soldiers who had fought in the same place during World War I. The Justice League United arrives to try to fix the problem, and Sergeant Rock ends up leading a strange company of combatants that includes Super Heroes and a German flying ace.

VITAL STATS

REAL NAME Franklin Rock

OCCUPATION Soldier

HEIGHT 6 ft (1.83 m)

WEIGHT 183 lb (83 kg)

BASE Pittsburgh, Pennsylvania

MAIN ALLIES Easy Company

MAIN FOES Vandal Savage

THE SEVEN DEADLY SINS
VICES MADE FLESH

The Seven Deadly Sins are demonic manifestations of the worst sins of humankind. They are captured by the wizard Shazam and trapped in stone statues. However, they are later released and come into the possession of the wicked Black Adam. Shazam believes that Pride is the most dangerous of all the Sins.

SIN BEAST

Black Adam has control over the Seven Deadly Sins, who must follow his orders. He sends them all to possess a single human at once in order to try to force Shazam to give his magic to Adam. Their actions create a giant beast that rampages through the streets, putting everything in danger. When Black Adam is defeated, the Sins are free and they leave the human that they have possessed.

MEMBERS INCLUDE

1. PRIDE
2. GLUTTONY
3. ENVY
4. GREED
5. WRATH
6. LUST
7. SLOTH

SHAZAM
EARTH'S MIGHTIEST MORTAL

Teenager Billy Batson is chosen by an ancient wizard to receive the powers of Shazam. When Billy speaks the magic word, he transforms into an adult, and an incredibly strong and powerful hero. His magical abilities then grant him the wisdom of Solomon, the strength of Hercules, the stamina of Atlas, the power of Zeus, the courage of Achilles, and the speed of Mercury.

Hooded cloak is in keeping with the mystical nature of Shazam's powers

POWERS

As Shazam, Billy Batson is a master of the Living Lightning, able to direct powerful energy blasts at opponents. He can fly, has superhuman strength and stamina, and is virtually indestructible. He is also Magic's Champion, able to cast spells, often by using his own name as a magic word—"Shazam!"

Lightning symbol represents the Living Lightning

NEW TRICKS

After the death of the evil god Darkseid, Billy's connection to the power of the old gods is gone. With the help of his wizard mentor, Billy meets new deities whose powers he will now wield instead. He proves to them that he is worthy of their awesome powers by defeating Zonuz, the father of Darkseid. Shazam is now even more powerful than before.

VITAL STATS

REAL NAME Billy Batson

OCCUPATION Super Hero

HEIGHT 6 ft 2 in (1.88 m)

WEIGHT 220 lb (100 kg)

BASE Philadelphia, Pennsylvania

MAIN ALLIES The Shazam Family, Justice League

MAIN FOES Black Adam, Doctor Sivana

SHAZAM FAMILY
MARVELOUS MAGICAL SIBLINGS

Billy Batson's foster family can share his power of Shazam whenever he chooses. As foster siblings taken in by the kindly Victor and Rosa Vásquez, the young people have a close bond, making them an ideal team. The Shazam Family knows that a real family is about more than just blood ties.

FIGHTING TOGETHER

When the evil Black Adam gets ahold of Billy's foster siblings and demands that Billy give the power of Shazam to him, Billy realizes that he can instead give his abilities to his family. Dressed in similar costumes, with almost identical powers, the Shazam Family takes down Black Adam, although it is Billy who ends up delivering the final blow.

MEMBERS INCLUDE

1. EUGENE CHOI Eugene can communicate with machinery.

2. DARLA DUDLEY Darla has super-speed.

3. BILLY BATSON Shazam can bestow his superpowers on others.

4. FREDDY FREEMAN Freddy shares all of Shazam's superpowers.

5. PEDRO PEÑA Pedro is super-strong.

6. MARY BROMFIELD Much like Freddy, Mary can use all of Shazam's powers.

SIDEWAYS
RIFT JUMPER

High-school student Derek James is an unremarkable teenager, until a visit to Gotham City exposes him to the Dark Multiverse and leaves him with amazing new powers. Confiding in his best friend Ernie, Derek adopts a costume and the name Sideways, hoping to become a Super Hero. However, his new powers can be very dangerous, and he is about to enter a strange new reality—or several realities.

POWERS

After being exposed to the energy of the Dark Multiverse, Sideways is able to open portals, which he calls rifts, with his fingers and jump through them to other places. He also has super-strength as a side effect. Without proper training, though, his jumping could cause problems with the fabric of reality itself.

The symbol on Sideways's mask is the same shape as the rifts he opens

VITAL STATS

REAL NAME Derek James

OCCUPATION High-school student

HEIGHT 5 ft 7 in (1.70 m)

WEIGHT 148 lb (67 kg)

BASE North Gotham City

MAIN ALLIES Ernie, Tempus Fuginaut

MAIN FOES Killspeed, Replicant, Showman

NEW REALITY

Coming home one day, Sideways encounters a mysterious alien being, cramming his giant frame into Derek's bedroom. This alien, named Tempus Fuginaut, shows Derek the home of the Fuginauts, a time between times and a place between places. He tells the confused teen that Derek is now uniquely placed to protect his own reality.

Sideways's costume is made by his friend Ernie, a keen cosplayer

THE SIGNAL
BATMAN'S PROTEGÉ

Batman takes young Duke Thomas under his wing to train him, not as another Robin, but as something new. Duke becomes the Signal, a hero for Gotham City's daylight hours. He sees the city in a different way, partly thanks to his metahuman light powers, and Batman believes he is the perfect partner to give Gotham City protection when the other Bats are sleeping.

The Signal's high-tech suit contains an electrical charge defense system and a stealth mode

The Signal prefers to fight with escrima sticks like some other Bat-Family members

THE SIGNAL'S SECRET BASE

When Batman tells Duke to meet in a secret room beneath the Fox Center, the Signal has no idea what is in store. Duke is shocked to discover that Batman has had a secret base built for him, which he calls the Hatch. The base contains computers, gym equipment, an upgraded suit, and a customized yellow motorcycle that can turn invisible.

POWERS

Unlike most of the Bat-Family, the Signal has metahuman powers. His eyes can process light more quickly than others can, and he can even sense where light has been and where it will be. This gives the Signal the ability to see events a few minutes into the past or into the future.

SINESTRO
FEAR-WIELDER

Originally from the planet Korugar (since destroyed), Sinestro is a former Green Lantern who helped train Hal Jordan. Now, he wears a yellow power ring as master of the emotion of fear and leads his own Corps, named in his honor. Sinestro seeks to use fear to bring the universe to order. He is one of the Green Lantern Corps's most powerful and dangerous foes.

VITAL STATS

REAL NAME Thaal Sinestro

OCCUPATION Leader of Sinestro Corps, super-villain

HEIGHT 6 ft 7 in (2.01 m)

WEIGHT 204 lb (92 kg)

BASE Qward

MAIN ALLIES Sinestro Corps, Parallax, Black Adam

MAIN FOES Green Lantern Corps

Magenta skin is characteristic of Korugarians

SINESTRO SAVES EARTH

When powerful fanatics The Paling try to invade Earth, Sinestro arrives to save the planet. He temporarily recruits several of Earth's heroes and villains into the Sinestro Corps to help him. When the day is saved, an exhausted Sinestro cannot help but enjoy the unusual sensation of being a hero to the people of Earth.

Yellow power ring is fueled by fear

POWERS

Sinestro wields the power of fear and has a supreme understanding of it even without his power ring. The ring, made by Weaponers on the planet Qward, enables him to fly and create energy constructs. As a former Green Lantern, he also has incredible willpower.

SOLOMON GRUNDY
WALKING DEAD

In life, Cyrus Gold is a 19th-century criminal who dies in Slaughter Swamp, Gotham City. But death is not the end, and the unusual properties of the swamp cause him to rise again as the zombie Solomon Grundy. Grundy says nothing except the nursery rhyme he is named after. He is one of the heavy-hitters recruited by Amanda Waller into the Suicide Squad offshoot team—Task Force XL.

Solomon Grundy's flesh is deathly pale in color

Grundy's suit is the one he wore in life, back in the 19th century

ZOMBIE VS. CLONE

Grundy is freed from prison by a mysterious benefactor, who tells Grundy that he will stay free if he causes chaos in Gotham City. Two Outlaws team members—Red Hood and Artemis—try to stop the rampaging zombie, but Grundy is too much for them. They are saved by their teammate Bizarro, who rises from his sickbed to take Grundy down, at great cost to himself.

POWERS

Solomon Grundy has superhuman strength and stamina and can hold his own against the strongest Super Heroes in a fight. Even if he is killed, Grundy can rise again, sometimes with a different personality and increased or reduced intellect compared to his previous incarnation.

VITAL STATS

REAL NAME Cyrus Gold
OCCUPATION Super-villain
HEIGHT 9 ft 2 in (2.79 m)
WEIGHT 971 lb (440 kg)
BASE Slaughter Swamp, Gotham City
MAIN ALLIES The Joker, Task Force XL
MAIN FOES Batman, The Outlaws

THE SPECTRE
AGENT OF VENGEANCE

The Spectre is appointed to be an agent of justice by the all-powerful Presence. His brand of justice is unforgiving, and he punishes the guilty harshly. The Spectre's human host is Detective Jim Corrigan of Gotham City, a place where there is no shortage of guilty people to bring justice to.

VITAL STATS

REAL NAME James "Jim" Corrigan

OCCUPATION Bringer of Justice, police detective

HEIGHT 6 ft 1 in (1.85 m)

WEIGHT 184 lb (83 kg)

BASE Gotham City

MAIN ALLIES Justice Society of America

MAIN FOES Phantom Stranger

As the Spectre, Corrigan's skin is pale

Jim Corrigan wears a green, hooded cloak to conceal his identity

POWERS

The Spectre is one of the most powerful beings in existence, although he needs a human host in order to function. He is all but invulnerable to everything except very powerful magic. He is capable of incredible feats of strength and sorcery that can alter reality itself.

THE VOICE OF DOG

When the Phantom Stranger bursts in on The Spectre, accusing him of taking his family, the situation escalates, and the two mighty beings are soon fighting. They are stopped by the sound of the all-powerful Voice who gave them their powers. Voice chides them like naughty schoolchildren from the body of a Scottish Terrier dog.

SPOILER
THE VILLAIN'S DAUGHTER

Spoiler, a.k.a. Stephanie Brown, has an unusual start in the world of Super Heroes. She is the daughter of lesser-known villain Cluemaster, and decides to do the right thing by "spoiling" his evil plans. As Spoiler, she goes on to become a vigilante in Gotham City and a member of the Bat-Family of heroes.

POWERS

Spoiler does not have metahuman powers, but is highly skilled in acrobatics and martial arts. She has been trained by both Batgirl and Catwoman, as well as Batwoman and Batman as part of The Gotham Knights team. She is also a skilled computer hacker.

Spoiler is skilled in the use of grappling hooks

Like many other members of the Bat-Family, Spoiler wears a gadget-packed Utility Belt

DEFEATING DAD

Cluemaster and Spoiler clash in a fight set up by the villain Hush. Spoiler escapes her father on a motorcycle, but he pursues her, throwing an explosive at her cycle. Just as she is performing a motorcycle jump in midair, the bomb goes off! Luckily, Spoiler leaps to safety, and the police—who she called in advance—arrive to arrest her father.

VITAL STATS

REAL NAME Stephanie Brown

OCCUPATION Vigilante

HEIGHT 5 ft 5 in (1.65 m)

WEIGHT 110 lb (50 kg)

BASE Gotham City

MAIN ALLIES The Bat-Family

MAIN FOES Mother, Anarky, Brother Eye

STAR SAPPHIRE
THE POWER OF LOVE

Carol Ferris is a member of the Star Sapphire Corps, wielding a ring powered by the light of love. Although at first she struggles to control her emotions as a Star Sapphire, Carol eventually becomes one of the greatest wielders of the violet light. She tries to balance her life as a hero with her responsibilities of running her family business, Ferris Aircraft.

VITAL STATS

REAL NAME Carol Ferris

OCCUPATION Star Sapphire, businesswoman

HEIGHT 5 ft 7 in (1.70 m)

WEIGHT 125 lb (57 kg)

BASE Coast City, California; Zamaron

MAIN ALLIES Star Sapphire Corps, Green Lantern Corps

MAIN FOES Relic, Volthoom

POWERS

Star Sapphire has a violet power ring, which she can use to fly and create hard-light constructs. She can also deploy a "heart tether" to take her to join someone she loves anywhere in the universe, or to take her somewhere where love itself is threatened.

When Star Sapphire is using her powers, her eyes appear completely white

TUG OF LOVE

Carol is surprised when she is suddenly teleported to the far side of the universe. The Guardians of the Universe have figured out how to hack Carol's Star Sapphire ring and need her help. She must rescue Kyle Rayner from a being named Relic, who is learning the Green Lantern Corps's secrets from his mind. Carol uses her power to call Kyle to her, freeing him from Relic's control.

Star Sapphire's costume is violet, the color of love on the emotional spectrum

STARFIRE
ALIEN PRINCESS

Starfire comes to Earth after escaping captivity on her home planet of Tamaran. With her instinct to help people and her incredible superpowers, she is a natural Super Hero. Starfire is a longstanding member of the Teen Titans. Later, she joins a division of the Justice League formed to travel through space searching for problems caused by the breaking of the Source Wall—the barrier encasing the Multiverse.

Starfire's eyes are green and pupilless, typical of a native of Tamaran

NOBODY'S PRISONER

Starfire is captured by the Psions, alien scientists who will use any means, including violence, to increase their knowledge. They have studied her before and want to know how much her power has increased since then. But Starfire was once a prisoner on Tamaran, and she promises herself that she will never be captured again. She summons all her power and bursts out of the Psions' restraints.

When Starfire uses her abilities, her hair has the illusion of turning to fire

VITAL STATS

REAL NAME Koriand'r
OCCUPATION Super Hero
HEIGHT 6 ft 4 in (1.93 m)
WEIGHT 158 lb (72 kg)
BASE Mobile
MAIN ALLIES Justice League, Teen Titans, Blackfire
MAIN FOES Deathstroke, The Citadel

POWERS

Starfire's powers appear after she is experimented on while a prisoner. She can absorb solar radiation and fire it out as energy blasts, which she calls "Starbolts." She can fly and has super-strength, stamina, and durability. Starfire is also trained in combat by the warlords of Okaara while still on Tamaran.

STARGIRL
CELEBRITY SUPER HERO

Based in Los Angeles, Stargirl is a Super Hero with an army of adoring teenage fans. She is only a teenager herself and still attends high school, but her possession of the powerful Cosmic Staff allows her to save lives when she's not studying. Stargirl always faces great danger with a smile on her face.

Although Stargirl wears a mask, many people know her true identity

SUPER FRIENDS

When Martian Manhunter gets trapped inside a prison containing the Justice League, only Stargirl can help him escape. The prison uses the weaknesses and fears of its inmates to keep them confined, but Stargirl's youthful optimism makes her almost immune to it. After she and Martian Manhunter escape, they form a close friendship and are often found looking out for one another on missions.

VITAL STATS

REAL NAME Courtney Whitmore
OCCUPATION Student
HEIGHT 5 ft 5 in (1.65 m)
WEIGHT 137 lb (62 kg)
BASE Los Angeles, California
MAIN ALLIES Justice League United, Justice League of America
MAIN FOES Despero

POWERS

Stargirl's powers come from her equipment—the Cosmic Staff uses the absorbed energy of stars to enable her to fly, create force fields, and fire energy blasts. Stargirl also has the Cosmic Converter Belt, which gives her super-strength, speed, agility, and stamina.

Stargirl's belt and staff previously belonged to the Justice Society hero Starman

STARMAN
A HEROIC LEGACY

Jack Knight inherits the heroic identity of Starman from his brother, who in turn had taken over from their father. Although Jack never intends to become a Super Hero, wanting only to run his antiques and collectibles store, he takes up the Cosmic Rod and defends his beloved Opal City as the new Starman.

VITAL STATS

REAL NAME Jack Knight

OCCUPATION Antiques store owner, Super Hero

HEIGHT 6 ft 1 in (1.85 m)

WEIGHT 165 lb (75 kg)

BASE Opal City

MAIN ALLIES Justice Society of America, Stargirl, The O'Dare family

MAIN FOES The Mist

Jack Knight wears tank driver goggles to protect his eyes from the energy of the Cosmic Rod

SAND AND STARS

Starman visits one of his father's elderly former Justice Society teammates, Sandman, and they uncover a plot to sabotage an airship launch. Sandman, despite his frailty, dons his old mask and gas gun to rescue Starman when he is captured by the crooks. Once freed, Starman uses the Cosmic Staff to zoom into the air and save the airship's passengers from disaster.

Starman wields the Cosmic Rod, an artifact of great power

POWERS

As part of the Starman legacy, Jack inherits the Cosmic Rod. This is powered with energy from the stars and gives him the ability to fly. It also creates force fields and absorbs energy, which can be fired in powerful blasts. Jack is also trained in the martial art of Jujutsu.

STARRO
TELEPATHIC ALIEN STARFISH

An alien tyrant of unknown origin, Starro resembles a giant Earth starfish. However, unlike the marine creature, Starro intends to conquer the universe. He tries to do this by taking control of people's minds. After multiple defeats by various heroes, Starro reemerges with a new personality and even a possible tendency toward heroism.

Limbs can be regenerated if lost

POWERS

Starro is able to use mind control on other beings. Originally he did this by creating smaller parasitic copies of himself to attach to victims' faces, but he is now able to use mind control directly. Starro is also able to fly, even through space, and is incredibly durable.

Starro has a single giant eye, like his miniature copies

VITAL STATS

REAL NAME Starro

OCCUPATION Conqueror

HEIGHT 32 ft (9.75 m)

WEIGHT 6,000 lb (2,722 kg)

BASE Mobile

MAIN ALLIES Duplicate spores of himself

MAIN FOES Justice League

STARRO SACRIFICES HIMSELF

Starro becomes a hero when he is recruited by Brainiac into an unlikely team-up of various heroes and villains. Their mission is to save the planet Colu from a giant Omega Titan. Starro attaches himself to the face of the Titan to distract it, only to be torn apart.

Natasha Irons follows the family tradition when she takes up the heroic identity of Steel, also used by her uncle, John Henry Irons. Steel is inspired by Superman to protect Metropolis, and the Ironses use the incredible tech in their Steelworks lab to create battle suits. Natasha's tech knowledge makes her a massive asset to the Titans team.

POWERS

Natasha has a genius-level intellect, particularly in the fields of engineering and computing. She creates her own battle armor, which gives her the power of flight, as well as super-strength and durability. Like her uncle, Natasha wields a kinetic hammer as her weapon.

Like her uncle before her, Steel wears an S-shield on her armor to show she is part of the Superman Family

The chrome that forms Steel's armor is semisentient, and forms around her at her command

HOME-MAKING

When Steel is recruited to the new Titans lineup, she goes with the others to settle into their new base. The other Titans are disappointed to find an empty room, but Steel wanted it to be that way. Revealing a tiny metal cube, she strikes it with her kinetic hammer. Everything they need for their missions miraculously bursts out of the cube and furnishes the room.

VITAL STATS

REAL NAME Natasha Irons

OCCUPATION Super Hero

HEIGHT 5 ft 6 in (1.68 m)

WEIGHT 106 lb (48 kg)

BASE Metropolis

MAIN ALLIES Titans, John Henry Irons, Lana Lang

MAIN FOES Lex Luthor, Mercy Graves

STEPPENWOLF
LORD OF BATTLE

Steppenwolf is not only Darkseid's ferocious war general but also his uncle. He does not command from a safe distance but instead fights in the front lines, leading Apokoliptian forces such as Dog Cavalry or Parademons. He has, however, been known to question Darkseid's orders and even look for glory for himself.

POWERS

Steppenwolf is a New God and therefore super-strong, fast, and durable. As the leader of the armies of Apokolips, he is a superb fighter, trained over countless years in both armed and unarmed combat. Steppenwolf is also an expert animal trainer from his command of the Dog Cavalry.

Horned helmet makes Steppenwolf stand out on the battlefield

Though master of many weapons, Steppenwolf prefers the incredibly powerful Electro Ax

KING STEPPENWOLF

After leading an invasion of Earth-2, Steppenwolf is forced to go into hiding there. He makes a comeback when his daughter, Fury, helps him overthrow the ruler of the kingdom of Dherain. Steppenwolf names himself as the new king. But his grab for personal glory does not go down well with those loyal to Darkseid, and he is defeated.

VITAL STATS

REAL NAME Steppenwolf

OCCUPATION Military Commander of Apokolips

HEIGHT 6 ft 9 in (2.06 m)

WEIGHT 330 lb (150 kg)

BASE Apokolips

MAIN ALLIES Darkseid, Fury

MAIN FOES Mister Miracle, Big Barda

STEVE TREVOR
AGENT OF A.R.G.U.S.

Steve Trevor is washed up on Themyscira as the first ever visitor from "Man's World." He is found by Diana, Princess of the Amazons, and the two become close. Diana is chosen to accompany Trevor back home, where he helps her adjust to her new life as Wonder Woman, and also sometimes helps her on missions.

When on secret missions, Trevor must rely only on what he can carry in his backpack

Steve Trevor's girlfriend, Wonder Woman, is not a fan of his new beard

THE ODDFELLOWS

Steve commands a secret A.R.G.U.S. task force called the Oddfellows. Some of their missions are so covert that even most A.R.G.U.S. employees are unaware of them. On one occasion, the rest of the Oddfellows signal Trevor for help when they are captured. Chief, one of the Oddfellows, has made a strange fish-shaped necklace for Steve. At a key moment, he tells Steve it is actually a bomb, and Steve hurls it into the air to cause a distraction and aid their escape.

POWERS

Steve Trevor has no superpowers; but as a highly trained member of the US military, he is skilled in firearms use, tactics, and hand-to-hand combat. Having taken part in countless covert missions, Trevor is also a master of stealth, and has tremendous courage.

Task Force X—otherwise known as the Suicide Squad—is a super-secret government force made up almost entirely of criminals. The team is run by Amanda Waller, who has complete control over the team members, thanks to implants in their heads. She can give them a shock, or worse, if they do not follow her orders. The squad operates out of Belle Reve Penitentiary and performs well on their classified missions.

MEMBERS INCLUDE

1. RICK FLAG Rick is a veteran soldier, who keeps the villains in line.

2. KATANA This elite warrior freely chooses to join the squad.

3. KILLER CROC The monstrous Croc finds a family of sorts with Task Force X.

4. HARLEY QUINN Fun-loving Harley surprises the team with her leadership qualities.

5. CAPTAIN BOOMERANG "Digger" is one of the longest-serving squad members.

6. DEADSHOT The world's best killer-for-hire is a munitions expert.

7. ENCHANTRESS This evil sorceress is trapped in the body of an innocent graphic designer.

SQUAD SHUTDOWN

The US super-soldier code named The Wall arrives at Belle Reve with orders to take out the villain Hack and shut down Task Force X. Following his mission, The Wall goes rogue, holding everyone in Washington, D.C. hostage. The Suicide Squad is sent in and manages to stop him. Afterward, the president allows the team to remain operational.

SUPERBOY
SON OF SUPERMAN

Born in the Fortress of Solitude, Jonathan Kent is the son of Superman and Lois Lane. Jon develops powers like his father as he gets older, and his parents realize they must guide and help their son to deal with his unique physiology. Jon wants to be a hero just like Superman, but he also needs to learn how to be himself.

POWERS

Jon's powers are very similar to his father's: he can fly and has heat vision, freeze breath, super-strength, speed, and durability. Jon also has an advanced healing factor. However, because Jon is half-human, his powers may develop differently from his father's as he grows. He sometimes also has trouble controlling them.

SPACE ODYSSEY

Jon is troubled by a vision of the future in which his powers hurt people, so he decides that he wants to go with his grandfather, Jor-El, on a trip across the galaxy. Jor-El thinks that learning more about what is beyond Earth will help his grandson. Although at first Jon's parents refuse, they come to see that the trip will help their son, and Lois decides to go, too.

VITAL STATS

REAL NAME Jonathan Samuel "Jon" Kent

OCCUPATION Student, Super Hero

HEIGHT 4 ft 6 in (1.37 m)

WEIGHT 84 lb (38 kg)

BASE Metropolis

MAIN ALLIES Superman, Lois Lane, Robin (Damian Wayne)

MAIN FOES The Eradicator

Superboy wears a jacket bearing the House of El symbol

Superboy welded his cape to his jacket himself using heat vision

SUPERGIRL
GIRL OF STEEL

Kara Zor-El is sent to Earth as a teenager by her father when her home city on Krypton is doomed to destruction. Her escape pod crash-lands on Earth, where she discovers her cousin Kal-El, who is now the hero Superman. Kara gains powers like his and becomes a Super Hero known as Supergirl. However, she struggles to fit in and also finds it hard at first to control her powers.

Like her cousin, Supergirl wears red and blue, adorned with the symbol of the House of El

POWERS

Supergirl's powers are the same as any Kryptonian under Earth's yellow sun—she can fly, use heat vision and freeze breath, and has super-strength, speed, and durability. She can also use her scream as a sonic weapon. Kara is vulnerable to Kryptonite and magic.

VITAL STATS

REAL NAME Kara Zor-El

OCCUPATION Super Hero

HEIGHT 5 ft 5 in (1.65 m)

WEIGHT 120 lb (54 kg)

BASE National City, California

MAIN ALLIES The Superman Family, Batgirl

MAIN FOES Brainiac, Cyborg Superman, Rogol Zaar

FAMILY REUNION

Supergirl is shocked to discover a Cyborg Superman inside the Fortress of Solitude. Worse still, he reveals that he is her father, Zor-El. He tells her that he saved Argo City—their hometown—from Krypton's destruction and that her mother is there. Kara has to find out if he is telling the truth. She finds Argo City out in space but discovers that her mother and the other citizens are cyborgs.

SUPER-MAN
CHINA'S MAN OF STEEL

Arrogant Kong Kenan is picked to be China's newest hero when he is seen scaring off a super-villain. Infused with the life force of a Kryptonian, he becomes Super-Man and a member of the Justice League of China. Kenan uses meditation to try to be a better person and a worthy Super Hero.

Super-Man's color scheme matches the flag of his homeland

SAVING SUPERMAN

Super-Man, unlike his Kryptonian namesake, does not count magic as a weakness, but a strength. During a fight against the Asura demigods, the combined powers of the American and Chinese Justice Leagues are only making their opponents stronger. Super-Man harnesses his qi energy to defeat them and save Superman from the magic of the evil All-Yang.

Super-Man's S-shield symbol features a representation of yin and yang, showing his mastery of inner balance

POWERS

Kong Kenan is imbued with an incredible range of powers similar to the original Superman's. At first Kenan cannot control his powers, but after he connects with the Red Jade Dragon artifact he is able to access them whenever he wants. Super-Man is the embodiment of yin and yang and is also able to use and resist magic.

SUPERMAN
MAN OF STEEL

Kal-El is sent to Earth as a baby when his home planet of Krypton is on the verge of destruction. He is found by farmers Jonathan and Martha Kent, who raise him as their son and name him Clark. As he grows, Clark discovers that he has amazing powers and begins to protect his adopted homeworld as Superman.

Superman's famous S-shield represents the House of El, and is also the Kryptonian sign meaning "hope"

A concealed button behind the belt buckle adjusts the suit to fit its wearer

SUPERMAN REVENGE SQUAD

Superman faces a challenge when several of his deadliest enemies decide to team up as the Superman Revenge Squad. Superman is joined by his own allies, including Supergirl, Superwoman, and Steel. The two sides engage in an epic battle, and the Revenge Squad almost wins, but the Man of Steel and his friends manage to defeat them.

POWERS

Superman's Kryptonian physiology gives him incredible powers when he is on a planet with a yellow sun, like Earth. He has super-strength, speed, stamina, and durability. Superman also has heat vision, X-ray vision, and super-hearing. He can fly and can even travel into space.

SWAMP THING
AVATAR OF THE GREEN

Alec Holland is chosen by the Parliament of Trees, a group of powerful beings dedicated to protecting nature, to become their avatar of the Green, the elemental force connecting all plant life on Earth. He is a mysterious Super Hero, often alone in the Louisiana bayou. However, when needed, he will answer the call from teams like the Justice League Dark, or even the Justice League itself.

Swamp Thing's green body is humanoid in shape but made entirely from plant material

Swamp Thing can grow or shrink his size through his control over the plant matter that makes up his body

POWERS

As avatar of the Green, Swamp Thing has total control over all plant life. He can rapidly grow branches or vines to subdue his enemies and can grow toxic plants to use as weapons. Swamp Thing is very strong and can even fly when he grows wing-shaped plants on his back.

ROTWORLD

When the Rot, the force of decay, has apparently conquered the world, Swamp Thing teams up with Animal Man, avatar of the Red, to try to put things right. The two discover that the Rot is actually a necessary part of life, but the corruption of Anton Arcane has taken it too far. Swamp Thing and Animal Man manage to restore the Earth's balance but at great personal cost to Swamp Thing and his beloved Abigail Arcane.

TALIA AL GHŪL
THE DEMON'S DAUGHTER

Talia al Ghūl is a lethal, skilled assassin and daughter of the demon Rā's al Ghūl. She is one of Batman's fiercest enemies, but the two have had romantic feelings for each other in the past. They even have a son together named Damian. Talia is a ruthless leader, who forms the villainous Leviathan Organization to defeat Batman and his allies.

Talia rules her vast criminal organization from a throne

Talia likes to wear elegant clothes

LIFE-GIVER

After Jason Todd's death at the hands of The Joker, it is Talia who brings him back to life using a mystical Lazarus Pit. She then puts him through rigorous training to become an elite assassin, but Jason turns his back on her and returns to Gotham City.

VITAL STATS

REAL NAME Talia al Ghūl

OCCUPATION Assassin

HEIGHT 5 ft 8 in (1.73 m)

WEIGHT 120 lb (54 kg)

BASE Mobile

MAIN ALLIES Rā's al Ghūl, League of Assassins, Leviathan Organization

MAIN FOES Batman

POWERS

Talia is a highly skilled hand-to-hand fighter in the tradition of the League of Assassins. However, she tries to conceal her prowess so that her enemies underestimate her. She is extremely intelligent and has access to the Lazarus Pits that have given her father immortality.

TEEN TITANS
SIDEKICKS NO MORE

Damian Wayne brings together the Teen Titans to help him see off the threat of Rā's al Ghūl's assassins. Despite Damian's controlling nature, the team bonds, and decides to stay together after the threat is passed. The Teen Titans are young heroes, still learning how to use their powers and make their way in the world. There is no doubt that whatever befalls them, together they are stronger.

MEMBERS INCLUDE

1. DJINN Djinn is a powerful genie who possesses a range of magical powers and is 4,000 years old.

2. ROUNDHOUSE This new face in the lineup is a human wrecking ball and social media star.

3. ROBIN The son of Batman, Damian Wayne, is sometimes a difficult leader.

4. RED ARROW Emiko Queen is Green Arrow's half sister and is also a highly trained assassin.

5. CRUSH The half-human, half-alien Crush has the same superpowers as her father, Lobo.

6. KID FLASH Wallace R. West is trying to forge a legacy of his own as Kid Flash.

SPEED FORCE SHOWDOWN

The Teen Titans team up with the Titans to stop Deathstroke when the villain manages to gain Speed Force powers. While Robin is happy to leave Deathstroke trapped inside the Speed Force, Kid Flash is not, and goes in after the villain with some of his allies. Deathstroke and the heroes return safely, but Robin is furious with Kid Flash and fires him from the team.

JUSTICE

TEMPEST
TITAN OF ATLANTIS

Garth was the first Aqualad but is now known as Tempest. He grew up under the guidance of Aquaman and trained in sorcery at the Silent School of Atlantis. Tempest is now a resident of the surface world and has joined the Titans team. He brings a wide range of abilities to the Titans, and in his team he finds friends for life.

Tempest's purple eyes mark him out as an Atlantean who has encyclopedic knowledge of his kingdom's history

VITAL STATS

REAL NAME Garth
OCCUPATION Super Hero
HEIGHT 5 ft 10 in (1.78 m)
WEIGHT 235 lb (107 kg)
BASE Titans Tower, New York City
MAIN ALLIES Titans, Aquaman, Mera
MAIN FOES Mister Twister, Deathstroke, Fearsome Five

POWERS

Tempest possesses all the incredible powers of an Atlantean: super-strength, speed, stamina, and durability, and of course the ability to live under water. In addition, Garth can use magic, although he has sworn not to following a tragedy in his school days. He can control water and create whirlpools at will.

MAGIC TOUCH

When Corum Rath takes the throne of Atlantis and traps the kingdom—and Aquaman—within a magical barrier, Mera asks Tempest to help her break through. Garth tries using his magic to tear it down. When this magical attempt fails, he tries a good old-fashioned fistfight, managing to snatch an amulet from a guard that will help Mera cross the barrier.

Atlantean armor is tough and durable

THUNDER AND LIGHTNING
FAMILY OF HEROES

Anissa and Jennifer Pierce are sisters with a special connection: they both have metahuman powers inherited from their father, Black Lightning. The siblings want to be heroes like their father, so Anissa takes the code name Thunder, and Jennifer calls herself Lightning. Although Black Lightning isn't happy about his daughters putting themselves in danger, there is no stopping Thunder and Lightning once they've made up their minds!

Keeping a promise to Black Lightning, Thunder does not put on her Super Hero costume until after she graduates from college

VITAL STATS

REAL NAME Anissa Pierce and Jennifer Pierce

OCCUPATION Super Heroes

HEIGHT 5 ft 7 in (1.70 m); 5 ft 5 in (1.65 m)

WEIGHT 119 lb (54 kg); 114 lb (52 kg)

BASE New York City; Chicago

MAIN ALLIES Outsiders, Black Lightning

MAIN FOES Shimmer, Doctor Chaos

THUNDER VS. LIGHTNING

Black Lightning, on the run from the law, is hoping to catch up with his two daughters. While Thunder is very happy to see him, Lightning and her Justice Society of America teammates want to do the right thing and take him into custody. The sisters' opposing views lead to a vicious fight between them. In the end, the spat is only ended by the intervention of the powerful Doctor Fate.

POWERS

Thunder can increase the density of her body, making her almost invulnerable. She can also use the increased density to cause shockwaves by stamping the ground. Lightning can absorb and store electrical energy, using it to fire out powerful blasts. She can also fly.

Lightning appears as a being made of pure electrical energy

TITANS
FRIENDS AND HEROES

The Titans is a super-team started by former members of the Teen Titans. Whatever the lineup, its members share a close bond of friendship and a desire to make their own way, independent of the Justice League. After the Source Wall is breached, Earth is covered in superpowered energy, and ordinary people start manifesting superpowers. The Titans make it their mission to find these people and help them deal with what is happening to them.

BOOM ROOM

The new Titans lineup faces its first mission in New York City, where there is a spike in superpowered energy. The team travels there in the Boom Room, built by team member Steel. This mobile command pod can also teleport. Then, the Titans ride out on motorcycles to investigate the mysterious energy readings.

MEMBERS INCLUDE

1. STEEL Natasha Irons is the team's tech guru as well as being a heavy hitter.

2. NIGHTWING Dick Grayson is a highly capable and brave team leader.

3. BEAST BOY Gar is an animal shape-shifter who likes telling jokes.

4. DONNA TROY This Super Hero is a highly trained Amazonian warrior.

5. MISS MARTIAN A powerful telepath, she is also the liaison with the Justice League.

6. RAVEN This empath also uses magical powers and is the daughter of a demon.

TOBIAS WHALE
HIGH-TECH GANGSTER

Tobias Whale is a gangster with a well-deserved bad reputation. Not content with the usual avenues of organized crime, Whale seeks the greater rewards found from breaking into the field of alien tech. He surrounds himself with metahuman accomplices to help fight off any unwanted attention from Super Heroes.

LIGHTNING STRIKES

Whale goes to Cleveland to introduce the locals to a special kind of gun, reverse-engineered from alien tech. He shows what his tech can do by causing chaos in the city. Whale intends to make a fortune selling the weapons to frightened citizens, but he does not plan for Black Lightning's involvement. The local hero outsmarts the villain and traps Whale in electrical bonds.

Whale's eyes appear totally black

Whale's sheer bulk is a useful weapon for keeping his crew in line

VITAL STATS

REAL NAME Tobias Whale

OCCUPATION Crime Lord

HEIGHT 6 ft 5 in (1.96 m)

WEIGHT 350 lb (159 kg)

BASE Los Angeles, California

MAIN ALLIES Miss Arquod, Sssear

MAIN FOES Black Lightning

POWERS

Tobias Whale has no superpowers, but seeks to rule the underworld through a combination of cunning and fear. His great size scares his opponents, and he is brutal in hand-to-hand combat. Whale is also a smart businessman, who figures out how to make crime pay.

THE TRICKSTER
CRIMINAL JOKESTER

The devious Trickster plagues Central City with his weaponized joke-store gadgets. He is an enemy of The Flash (Barry Allen) and teams up with the Rogues gang. However, the Trickster's volatile nature leads him to make some bad choices, and he sometimes even gets thrown out of the Rogues.

HEALING HAND

The Trickster betrays the Rogues gang to side with the Riddler in his attempted takeover of Central City. But he regrets his decision and rejoins the Rogues. He uses his newly enhanced robotic arm to heal Golden Glider and bring her out of her coma, with a little help from a sometime enemy The Flash (Barry Allen).

The Trickster's costume is a nod to his clownish personality

VITAL STATS

REAL NAME Axel Walker

OCCUPATION Criminal

HEIGHT 5 ft 7 in (1.70 m)

WEIGHT 150 lb (68 kg)

BASE Central City

MAIN ALLIES The Rogues

MAIN FOES The Flash (Barry Allen), Gorilla Grodd

POWERS

Although the Trickster does not have any superpowers, he is a genius inventor and mechanic, who constructs his range of joke-store gadgets. The Trickster also has an enhanced cybernetic arm, which replaced one that he lost in a confrontation with Gorilla Grodd.

The Trickster's anti-gravity boots enable him to fly for short periods of time

TRIGON
DEMONIC CONQUEROR

Trigon is an evil demon of immense power whose main ambition is to conquer every world that he finds. He also wants powerful children to continue his legacy and tries for countless years to father a child he considers worthy of his greatness. Finally he produces a daughter, Raven, who he believes could be his heir, but she rejects his evil.

Trigon can emit smoke from his horns

POWERS

Trigon's powers and size increase massively after he devours the Heart of Darkness, which stores the accumulated evils from 100 galaxies. He can open portals to access anywhere from his demonic realm. Trigon can shoot out fiery blasts of hellfire and can also control the minds of weaker beings to force them to follow him.

Trigon has several sets of eyes

VITAL STATS

REAL NAME Trigon

OCCUPATION Evil Demon

HEIGHT Variable

WEIGHT Variable

BASE The Under-Realms

MAIN ALLIES Church of Blood

MAIN FOES Teen Titans, Sons of Trigon

DEMON IN NEW YORK

Trigon arrives on Earth to enslave all of humanity, starting with New York City. All that stands in his way are the young heroes of the Teen Titans. However, the Teen Titans persuade his daughter Raven to join them, and together they drive Trigon off. The demon tells them that victory will be his in the end.

TWO-FACE
COIN-FLIPPING CRIMINAL

Harvey Dent, the boy who grows up to become Two-Face, is actually a friend of the young Bruce Wayne. However, after his face is horribly scarred, Harvey develops split personalities, with the deranged Two-Face side leading Harvey down a path of crime. Batman hopes that the good man Harvey once was can still be saved.

POWERS

Harvey Dent was a successful and intelligent attorney before he became Two-Face. He was also a friend of Batman, who trained Harvey in detective skills and martial arts. After Harvey's transformation into Two-Face, his many skills are instead channeled into criminal plots, often involving the number two.

Terribly disfigured in an attack by a criminal he helped convict, Two-Face's appearance shows his dual personalities

Two Face bases all his decisions on the flip of his special coin, which has one side scarred, like him

TWO-FACE FALLS

Harvey, Batman, and the Signal team up and try to find a possible cure for Harvey's condition. However, Two-Face doesn't want to be cured, so Batman has to tie him up. Being pursued by the Penguin, Black Mask, and King Shark, the heroes and Two-Face escape by plunging off a waterfall. Batman saves himself and Two-Face by using his cloak to glide down safely.

VITAL STATS

REAL NAME Harvey Dent

OCCUPATION Criminal, former lawyer

HEIGHT 6 ft (1.83 m)

WEIGHT 182 lb (83 kg)

BASE Gotham City

MAIN ALLIES Killer Moth, Firefly, Black Spider

MAIN FOES Batman, Robin

VANDAL SAVAGE
IMMORTAL EVIL

Vandal Savage becomes immortal when he touches a mysterious meteorite that has crashed into his Neanderthal world. During Savage's long life span, he turns his superior intellect to spreading evil throughout the world, planning eventually to rule it all. He claims to have had a hand in many of the most tragic events and eras of human history.

POWERS

Vandal Savage's only superhuman power is his immortality. However, over the course of millennia, he has honed all the skills he needs to become a super-villain. He is a master tactician and formidable warrior, who possesses the knack of persuading lesser beings to do his bidding.

Vandal Savage's Neanderthal background can still be traced in his modern-day appearance

SAVAGE DAWN

Vandal Savage gathers his descendants to help him draw the comet that gave him immortality back to Earth. He even removes Superman's powers to stop him from getting in his way. Once the comet's power is flowing through him, Savage thinks he's won, but Superman has managed to cure himself. The Man of Steel breaks the comet and, with it, Savage's new powers.

VITAL STATS

REAL NAME Vandar Adg

OCCUPATION Super-villain

HEIGHT 5 ft 10 in (1.78 m)

WEIGHT 176 lb (80 kg)

BASE Mobile

MAIN ALLIES Religion of Crime, Kassidy Savage, Secret Society of Super-Villains

MAIN FOES Justice Society of America, Superman, Pandora

VIXEN
MODEL HERO

Born in Zambesi, Mari McCabe inherits the Tantu Totem, a mystical artifact that enables her to access her hidden powers. At first, Mari embarks on a modeling and TV career, but she draws on the Totem's powers to rescue a kidnapped child. Mari realizes that she can make a real difference as the Super Hero Vixen, who can channel the abilities of any animal.

POWERS

Through the Tantu Totem, Vixen can access the Red—the elemental force that connects every form of animal life. Mari can take on an animal's abilities by speaking its name. She can even summon an accelerated healing factor by channeling the regenerative powers of the flatworm.

The Tantu Totem necklace links Vixen to her powers

Vixen's nails are super-strong and clawlike

HERO OF THE PEOPLE

The villain Prometheus confronts Vixen at the Justice League of America's headquarters. He accuses her of not caring about the public and secretly believing herself to be superior. When he threatens innocents, Vixen puts herself in danger to protect them. Prometheus is defeated with the League's help, and Vixen declares that ordinary people are better than heroes, as they face danger without powers.

VITAL STATS

REAL NAME Mari Jiwe McCabe

OCCUPATION Super Hero

HEIGHT 5 ft 9 in (1.75 m)

WEIGHT 140 lb (64 kg)

BASE The Sanctuary; Happy Harbor, Rhode Island

MAIN ALLIES Justice League of America, Batman

MAIN FOES Prometheus, Spiderbite

WEATHER WIZARD
STORM BRINGER

Marco Mardon comes from a family of criminals, but his weather-controlling powers make him very different from his relatives. He is taken in by a new "family," the Rogues gang, and they carry out heists around Central City. Naming himself Weather Wizard, Mardon brings his elemental powers to the Rogues' unending battles with The Flash (Barry Allen).

POWERS

Weather Wizard is the most powerful member of the Rogues. He can create and control any kind of weather and use air currents to fly. When Weather Wizard summons a thunderstorm, he can draw the electricity from inside it to fire lightning bolts at opponents.

Long coat is a key part of Weather Wizard's look

POWER OF THE HURRICANE

The Rogues try to protect Central City from the Secret Society of Super-Villains, following the invasion of Earth by the evil Crime Syndicate. When they seem to be facing defeat, they come up with a plan to send the Society to the alternate dimension named Mirror World, thanks to a ferocious hurricane summoned by Weather Wizard.

wOOOOOSHHHH

Staff through which Mardon channels his powers

VITAL STATS

REAL NAME Marco Mardon

OCCUPATION Criminal

HEIGHT 6 ft 1 in (1.85 m)

WEIGHT 184 lb (83 kg)

BASE Central City

MAIN ALLIES The Rogues

MAIN FOES The Flash (Barry Allen), Crime Syndicate, Gorilla Grodd

Diana is the princess of the Amazons of Themyscira, an all-female island nation. She travels to "Man's World" to use her god-given powers to make the whole planet a better place. Known as Wonder Woman, she is one of the Justice League's founding members. Her indomitable strength, endless compassion, and boundless courage are crucial to the team.

Tiara shows her status as a princess and is also a handy throwing weapon

Wristbands can deflect bullets

Lasso of Truth compels anyone to tell the truth

FRIEND AND ENEMY

Wonder Woman and Barbara Minerva were originally friends, until Barbara turned against Diana, blaming the hero for her transformation into The Cheetah. Diana needs Barbara's help to find her way back home. In exchange, The Cheetah demands assistance lifting the curse in order to return to her human self. They break the curse and then find a route back to Themyscira.

POWERS

Diana is given incredible powers by the Gods of Olympus, including super-strength, enhanced durability, super-speed, the ability to fly, and accelerated healing. She can also communicate with animals. As the greatest warrior of the Amazons, she is also a highly skilled fighter.

VITAL STATS

REAL NAME Diana

OCCUPATION Super Hero

HEIGHT 6 ft 2 in (1.88 m)

WEIGHT 148 lb (67 kg)

BASE Themyscira

MAIN ALLIES Justice League, Steve Trevor, Etta Candy

MAIN FOES The Cheetah, Ares, Veronica Cale, Darkseid, Grail

ZATANNA
MISTRESS OF MAGIC

Zatanna is a famous stage magician and daughter of the sorcerer John Zatara. Both are *Homo magi*—humans who can wield magic. She is a force for good and a member of the Justice League Dark. An ally of Batman, Zatana knows his secret identity and has known him since childhood.

Zatanna's costume is used both for her missions as a hero and her stage appearances as a magician

POWERS

Zatanna has honed her magical powers under the training of her father, Zatara. Her spells, cast by speaking the words backward, make her capable of almost anything. As well as using her amazing abilities to fight evil, Zatanna also uses them in her day job as a performer.

EDOLPXE

When Gotham City is threatened by Ascalon, a deadly A.I. created to replace the hero Azrael, Batman goes to Zatanna for help. She uses a powerful artifact, the Gnosis Sphere, to force the A.I. to stand down. She also destroys a rogue fleet of Batwing drones with a single word—"Edolpxe!"

VITAL STATS

REAL NAME Zatanna Zatara

OCCUPATION Magician

HEIGHT 5 ft 7 in (1.70 m)

WEIGHT 127 lb (58 kg)

BASE House of Mystery

MAIN ALLIES Justice League Dark, Batman

MAIN FOES Nick Necro, Felix Faust

H unter Zolomon is a former police profiler and friend of The Flash (Wally West), whose life is torn apart by tragedy. When Wally refuses to go back in time and change the past, Hunter becomes the speedster villain Zoom. He believes that he is making Wally a better hero by forcing him to suffer.

Zoom's eyes appear black-lensed with glowing red pupils

VITAL STATS

REAL NAME Hunter Zolomon

OCCUPATION Super-villain

HEIGHT 6 ft 1 in (1.85 m)

WEIGHT 181 lb (82 kg)

BASE Keystone City

MAIN ALLIES Reverse-Flash, Renegades, The Cheetah

MAIN FOES The Flash Family, Captain Cold

POWERS

Although a speedster, Zoom does not tap into the Speed Force, but instead alters the time around himself. This time manipulation gives him superhuman strength and speed. In addition, Zoom can create damaging sonic booms and shock waves with just a snap of his fingers.

FLASH WAR

Zoom is transported to the 25th century by Reverse-Flash but is left there alone. Hunter then lures the hero Wally West to him. He tells Wally that his children are still lost in the Speed Force, and the only way for Wally to rescue them is to break his connection to his powers. The fallout of Wally's decision causes a rift with his mentor, Barry Allen.

Zoom's costume closely resembles that of his ally, Reverse-Flash

Editor Matt Jones
Senior Editor David Fentiman
Senior Designer Anne Sharples
Project Art Editors Jon Hall, Jess Tapolcai
Pre-Production Producer Siu Yin Chan
Senior Producer Jonathan Wakeham
Managing Art Editor Vicky Short
Managing Editor Sadie Smith
Publisher Julie Ferris
Art Director Lisa Lanzarini
Publishing Director Simon Beecroft

First American Edition, 2019
Published in the United States by DK Publishing
1450 Broadway, Suite 801, New York, NY 10018

Page design copyright © 2019 Dorling Kindersley Limited
DK, a Division of Penguin Random House LLC

21 22 10 9 8 7 6

009–312635–Mar/2019

Published in Great Britain by Dorling Kindersley Limited.

A catalog record for this book is available from the Library of Congress.

ISBN: 978-1-46547-975-4

DK books are available at special discounts when purchased in bulk
for sales promotions, premiums, fund-raising, or educational use.
For details, contact: DK Publishing Special Markets,
1450 Broadway, Suite 801, New York, NY 10018
SpecialSales@dk.com

Printed and bound in China

A WORLD OF IDEAS:
SEE ALL THERE IS TO KNOW

www.dk.com
www.dccomics.com

DK would like to thank Amy Weingartner and Ashlea Green
at Warner Bros. Global Publishing; Doug Prinzivalli, Mike Pallotta,
and Leah Tuttle at DC Entertainment; Beth Davies, Julia March,
Jennette ElNaggar, Kayla Dugger, Lori Hand, Vicky Armstrong,
and Rosalyn Burton for editorial assistance; and Sunil Sharma
and Rajdeep Singh for design assistance.

Artists' Acknowledgments

Dan Abnett, ACO, Neal Adams, Tony Akins, Christian Alamy, Juan Albarran, Oclair Albert, Marlo Alquiza, Brad Anderson, Brent Anderson, Mirka Andolfo, Marc Andreyko, Roge Antonio, Ulises Arreola, Michael Atiyeh, Tony Aviña, Brian Azzarello, Barnaby Bagenda, Matt Banning, David Baron, Eddy Barrows, Sami Basri, Cary Bates, Chris Batista, Moose Baumann, Scott Beatty, Tony Bedard, Jordie Bellaire, Brian Michael Bendis, Ed Benes, Ryan Benjamin, Joe Bennett, Marguerite Bennett, Julie Benson, Shawna Benson, Rain Beredo, Jordi Bernet, BIT, W. Haden Blackman, Fernando Blanco, Blond, Jon Bogdanove, Viktor Bogdanovic, Tamra Bonvillain, Brett Booth, Alisson Borges, Brett Breeding, Philippe Briones, Amie Brockway-Metcalf, Daniel Brown, Brian Buccellato, Cullen Bunn, Chris Burnham, Buzz, Stephen Byrne, Jim Calafiore, Jamal Campbell, Greg Capullo, Eleanora Carlini, Pete Carlsson, Carmen Carnero, Keith Champagne, Bernard Chang, Jim Charalampidis, Bobbie Chase, Jim Cheung, Cliff Chiang, Brian Ching, June Chung, Vicente Cifuentes, Yıldıray Çınar, Matthew Clark, Andy Clarke, Martin Coccolo, Andre Coelho, Amanda Conner, Will Conrad, Andrew Constant, Gerry Conway, Darwyn Cooke, Paul Cornell, Mike Costa, Denys Cowan, Jeromy Cox, Chris Cross, Andrew Currie, Andrew Dalhouse, Tony S. Daniel, Sergio Davila, Marc Deering, Adam DeKraker, J.M. DeMatteis, Tom Derenick, Nick Derington, Hi-Fi Design, Carmine Di Giandomenico, Dan DiDio, Paul Dini, Terry Dodson, Christian Duce, Wes Dzioba, Dale Eaglesham, Scot Eaton, Neil Edwards, Gabe Eltaeb, Bilquis Evely, Nathan Eyring, Jason Fabok, Nathan Fairbairn, Romulo Fajardo, Jr., Wayne Faucher, Ray Fawkes, Riccardo Federici, Juan Fernandez, Raúl Fernández, Eber Ferreira, Julio Ferreira, Juan Ferreyra, Nick Filardi, David Finch, Brenden Fletcher, Sandu Florea, Shea Fontana, Gary Frank, Ron Frenz, Richard Friend, Jenny Frison, Veronica Gandini, Sunny Gho, Keith Giffen, Robert Gill, Aaron Gillespie, Jonathan Glapion, Adam Glass, Patrick Gleason, David S. Goyer, Justin Gray, Mick Gray, Devin Grayson, Dan Green, Tom Grummett, Ig Guara, Renato Guedes, Luis Guerrero, Yvel Guichet, Andres Guinaldo, Gene Ha, Larry Hama, Cully Hamner, Scott Hanna, Chad Hardin, Joe Harris, Tony Harris, Wes Hartman, Jeremy Haun, Andrew Hennessy, Daniel Henriques, Clayton Henry, Scott Hepburn, Jack Herbert, Phil Hester, Kyle Higgins, Bryan Hill, Bryan Hitch, Sandra Hope, Richard Horie, Tanya Horie, Jody Houser, Adam Hughes, Sam Humphries, Rob Hunter, Gregg Hurwitz, Mark Irwin, Tony Isabella, Jack Jadson, Mikel Janín, Klaus Janson, Van Jensen, Phil Jimenez, Jorge Jiménez, Geoff Johns, Casey Jones, J.G. Jones, Kelley Jones, Justin Jordan, Ruy José, Dan Jurgens, Kris Justice, John Kalisz, Gil Kane, Jeff Katz, Collin Kelly, Jessica Kholinne, Matt Kindt, Lovern Kindzierski, Jeff King, Tom King, Irene Koh, Scott Kolins, Tony Kordos, Andy Kubert, Joe Kubert, Aaron Kuder, Michel Lacombe, Stefano Landini, Andy Lanning, Jackson Lanzing, Serge LaPointe, Hope Larson, Ken Lashley, John Layman, Jim Lee, Jay Leisten, Jeff Lemire, Paul Levitz, Rob Liefeld, Steve Lightle, John Livesay, Scott Lobdell, Jeph Loeb, Rex Lokus, Matt Lopes, Aaron Lopresti, Marissa Louise, Adriano Lucas, Jose Luis,

Emanuela Lupacchino, Art Lyons, Andy MacDonald, Michelle Madsen, Doug Mahnke, Marcelo Maiolo, Guy Major, Francis Manapul, Clay Mann, Seth Mann, Guillem March, V. Ken Marion, Laura Martin, Roy Allan Martinez, Álvaro Martínez, Christy Marx, José Marzan, Jr., Thomas Mason, Nathan Massengill, Mike McAvennie, Dave McCaig, Ray McCarthy, Trevor McCarthy, Tom McCraw, Mike McKone, Shawn McManus, Lan Medina, Javier Mena, Jaime Mendoza, Jesús Merino, David Messina, Pop Mhan, Joshua Middleton, Danny Miki, Brian Miller, Peter Milligan, Inaki Miranda, Sula Moon, Mark Morales, Rags Morales, Tomeu Morey, Moritat, Grant Morrison, Amancay Nahuelpan, Jonboy Myers, J. Nanjan, Michael Alan Nelson, Diogenes Neves, Tom Nguyen, Jai Nitz, Ivan Nunes, Sonia Oback, Ben Oliver, Simon Oliver, Jerry Ordway, Steve Orlando, Carlo Pagulayan, Greg Pak, Tom Palmer, Jimmy Palmiotti, Eduardo Pansica, Peter Pantazis, Yanick Paquette, Jeff Parker, Sean Parsons, Allen Passalaqua, Tony Patrick, Jason Paz, Brent Peeples, Paul Pelletier, Benjamin Percy, George Pérez, Pere Pérez, Kate Perkins, Brandon Peterson, Hugo Petrus, Will Pfeifer, Khoi Pham, FCO Plascencia, Ivan Plascencia, Alberto Ponticelli, Francis Portela, Howard Porter, Joe Prado, Arif Prianto, Christopher Priest, Mark Propst, Steve Pugh, Jack Purcell, Wil Quintana, Rodney Ramos, Ron Randall, Norm Rapmund, John Rauch, Max Raynor, Brian Reber, Ivan Reis, Rod Reis, Dinei Ribeiro, Cliff Richards, Paul Rivoche, Andrew Robinson, James Robinson, Kenneth Rocafort, Robson Rocha, Carlos Rodriguez, Prentis Rollins, John Romita, Jr., Alex Ross, Riley Rossmo, Greg Rucka, Nei Ruffino, Jesús Saíz, Edgar Salazar, Tim Sale, Daniel Sampere, Alejandro Sanchez, Rafa Sandoval, Matt Santorelli, Elmer Santos, Marco Santucci, Otto Schmidt, Rob Schwager, Ethan Van Sciver, Mairghread Scott, Nicola Scott, Trevor Scott, Christopher Sebela, Tim Seeley, Stephen Segovia, Stjepan Šejić, John Semper, Jr., Declan Shalvey, Evan Shaner, Liam Sharp, Bill Sienkiewicz, Gail Simone, Alex Sinclair, Steve Skeates, Jeremiah Skipper, Cam Smith, Scott Snyder, Alex Sollazzo, Kevin Somers, Ryan Sook, Chris Sotomayor, Charles Soule, Dexter Soy, Mike Spicer, John Starr, Peter Steigerwald, Cameron Stewart, Karl Story, Goran Sudzuka, Ardian Syaf, Andre Szymanowicz, Marcio Takara, Billy Tan, Philip Tan, Babs Tarr, Jordi Tarragona, Tom Taylor, Art Thibert, Frank Tieri, Marcus To, Peter Tomasi, Wilfredo Torres, Sal Trapani, James Tynion IV, Le Beau Underwood, Carlos Urbano, Sarah Vaughn, Robert Venditti, José Villarrubia, Dexter Vines, Alessandro Vitti, Wade Von Grawbadger, Daniel Vozzo, Brennan Wagner, Mark Waid, Brad Walker, Gerard Way, Greg Weisman, Dean White, Bob Wiacek, Eric Wight, Chris Wildgoose, Rob Williams, Scott Williams, J.H. Williams III, Joshua Williamson, Bill Willingham, Matthew Wilson, Ryan Winn, Marv Wolfman, Pete Woods, Gregory Wright, Jason Wright, Jake Wyatt, Matt Yackey, Gene Luen Yang, and Patrick Zircher

The publishers have made every effort to identify and acknowledge the artists whose work appears in this *Guide*.